FINDER

Date	Day
Start Time	End Time
Location	
Temperature	Weather

Sketch	Directions (N S *p f*)	Intensity Estimates	Key
			0 = extremely bright 1 = bright areas 2 = general hue of disc 3 = shading near limit of visibility 4 = shading well seen 5 = unusually dark shading

Instrument	Seeing (Antoniadi Scale) I II III IV V
Magnification	Filters: W#
Sky very bright bright fair twilight dark	Transparency very good good fair poor
Phase Estimate: % filter W#	Disc Diameter
Illuminated Disc	Unilluminated Disc

FINDER

Date	Day
Start Time	End Time
Location	
Temperature	Weather

Sketch	Directions (N S *p f*)	Intensity Estimates	Key
			0 = extremely bright 1 = bright areas 2 = general hue of disc 3 = shading near limit of visibility 4 = shading well seen 5 = unusually dark shading

Instrument	Seeing (Antoniadi Scale) I II III IV V
Magnification	Filters: W#
Sky very bright bright fair twilight dark	Transparency very good good fair poor
Phase Estimate: % filter W#	Disc Diameter
Illuminated Disc	Unilluminated Disc

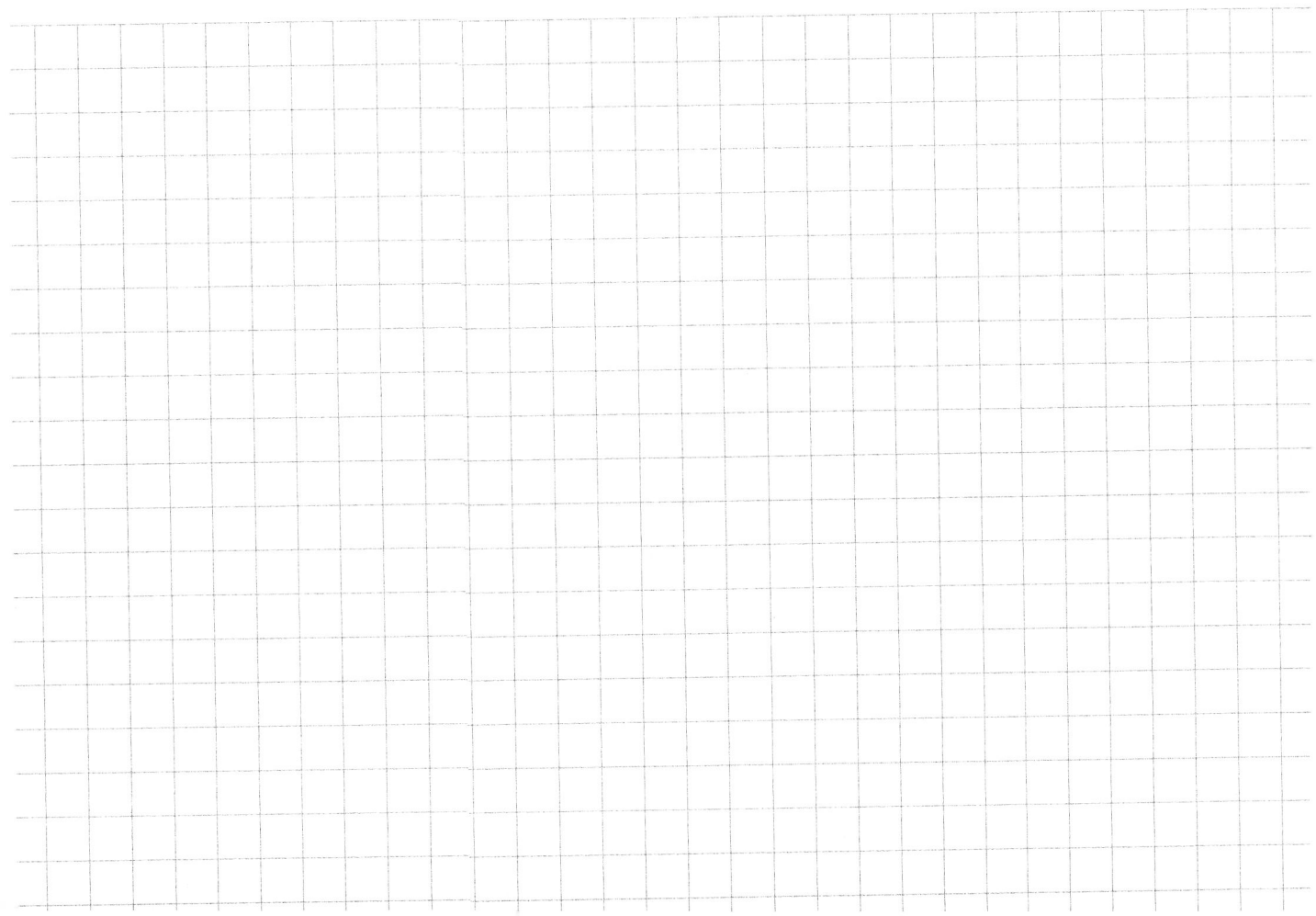

FINDER

Date		Day	
Start Time		End Time	
Location			
Temperature		Weather	

Sketch	Directions (N S *p f*)	Intensity Estimates	Key
	↕ ↔		0 = extremely bright 1 = bright areas 2 = general hue of disc 3 = shading near limit of visibility 4 = shading well seen 5 = unusually dark shading

Instrument	Seeing (Antoniadi Scale)
	I II III IV V
Magnification	Filters: W#
Sky very bright bright fair twilight dark	Transparency very good good fair poor
Phase Estimate: % filter W#	Disc Diameter
Illuminated Disc	Unilluminated Disc

FINDER

Date	Day
Start Time	End Time
Location	
Temperature	Weather

Sketch	Directions (N S *p f*)	Intensity Estimates	Key
	↕ ↔		0 = extremely bright 1 = bright areas 2 = general hue of disc 3 = shading near limit of visibility 4 = shading well seen 5 = unusually dark shading

Instrument	Seeing (Antoniadi Scale) I II III IV V
Magnification	Filters: W#
Sky very bright bright fair twilight dark	Transparency very good good fair poor
Phase Estimate: % filter W#	Disc Diameter
Illuminated Disc	Unilluminated Disc

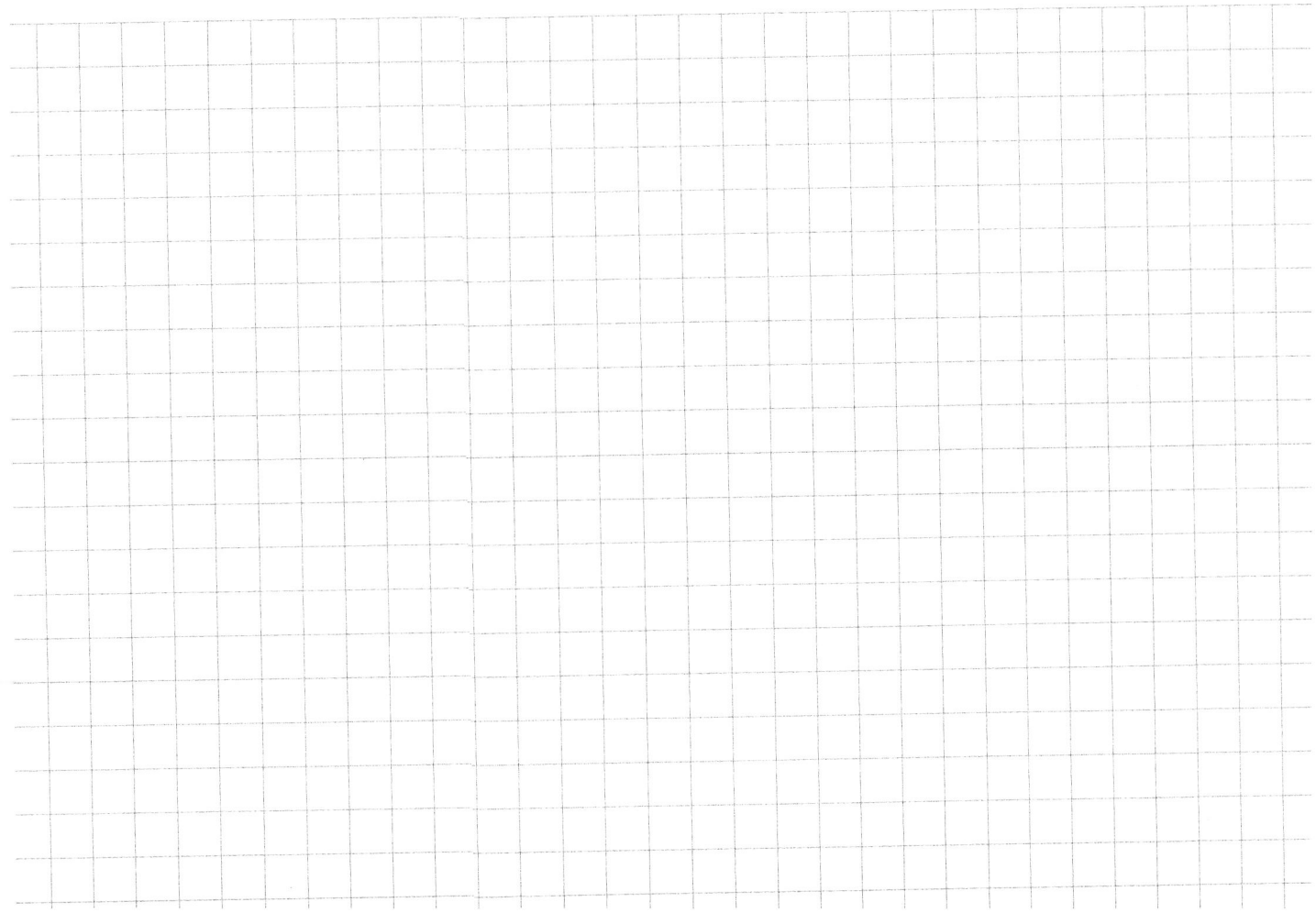

FINDER

Date		Day	
Start Time		End Time	
Location			
Temperature		Weather	

Sketch	Directions (N S *p f*)	Intensity Estimates	Key
	↕ ↔		0 = extremely bright 1 = bright areas 2 = general hue of disc 3 = shading near limit of visibility 4 = shading well seen 5 = unusually dark shading

Instrument	Seeing (Antoniadi Scale)
	I II III IV V
Magnification	Filters: W#
Sky very bright bright fair twilight dark	Transparency very good good fair poor
Phase Estimate: % filter W#	Disc Diameter
Illuminated Disc	Unilluminated Disc

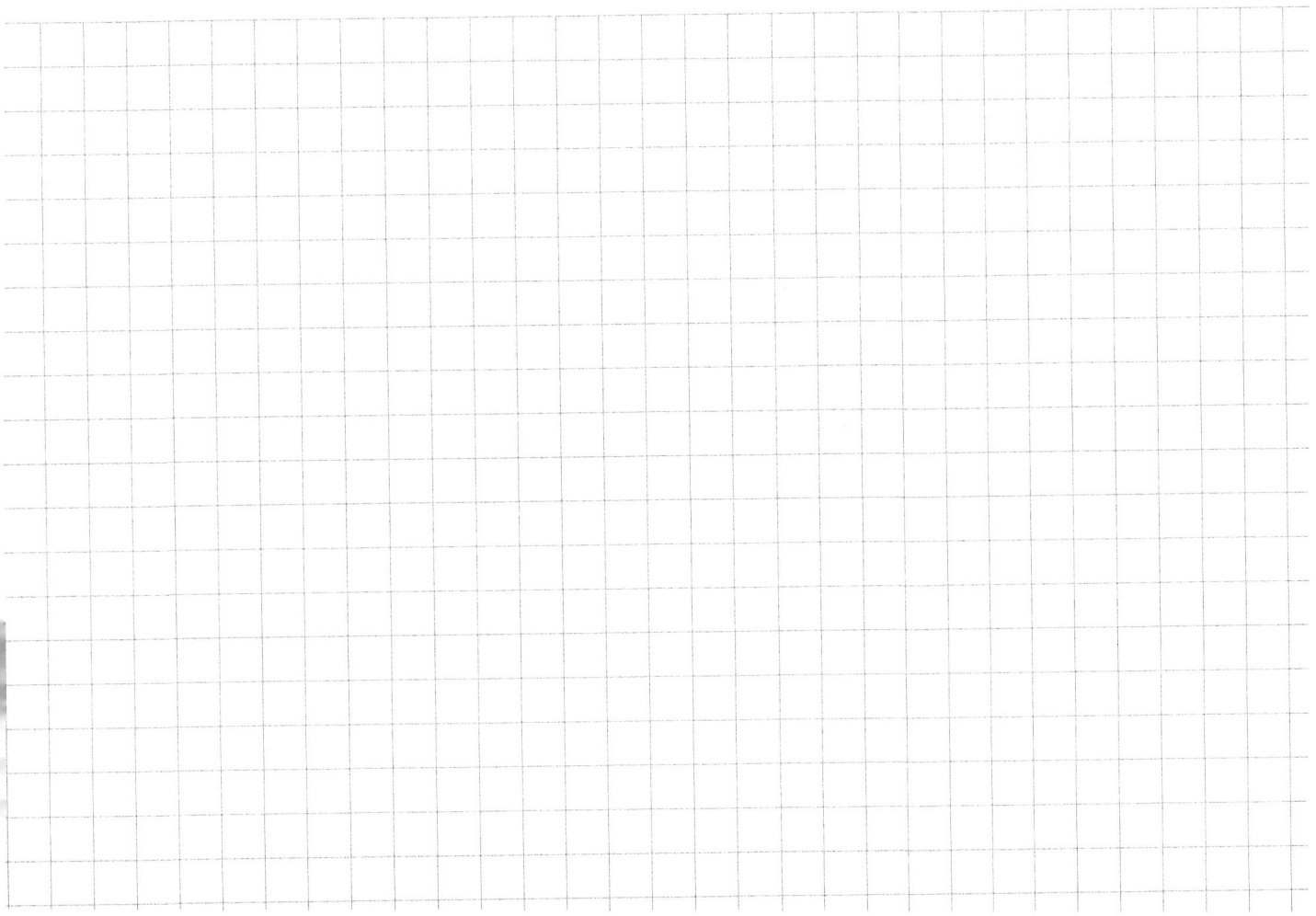

FINDER

Date	Day
Start Time	End Time
Location	
Temperature	Weather

Sketch	Directions (N S *p f*)	Intensity Estimates	Key
	↕ ↔		0 = extremely bright 1 = bright areas 2 = general hue of disc 3 = shading near limit of visibility 4 = shading well seen 5 = unusually dark shading

Instrument	Seeing (Antoniadi Scale) I II III IV V
Magnification	Filters: W#
Sky very bright bright fair twilight dark	Transparency very good good fair poor
Phase Estimate: % filter W#	Disc Diameter
Illuminated Disc	Unilluminated Disc

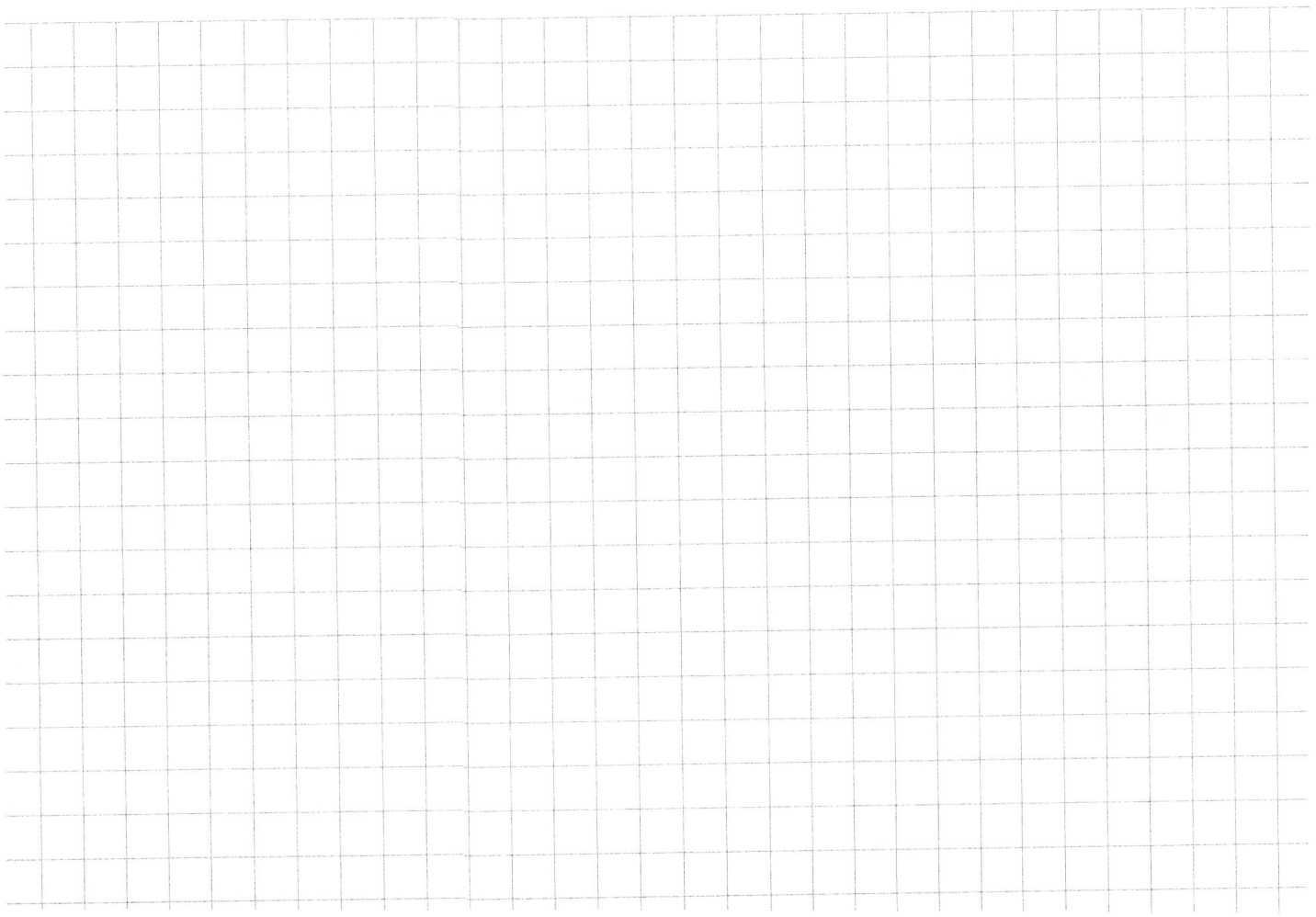

FINDER

Date		Day	
Start Time		End Time	
Location			
Temperature		Weather	

Sketch	Directions (N S *p f*)	Intensity Estimates	Key
			0 = extremely bright 1 = bright areas 2 = general hue of disc 3 = shading near limit of visibility 4 = shading well seen 5 = unusually dark shading

Instrument	Seeing (Antoniadi Scale)
	I II III IV V
Magnification	Filters: W#
Sky very bright bright fair twilight dark	Transparency very good good fair poor
Phase Estimate: % filter W#	Disc Diameter
Illuminated Disc	Unilluminated Disc

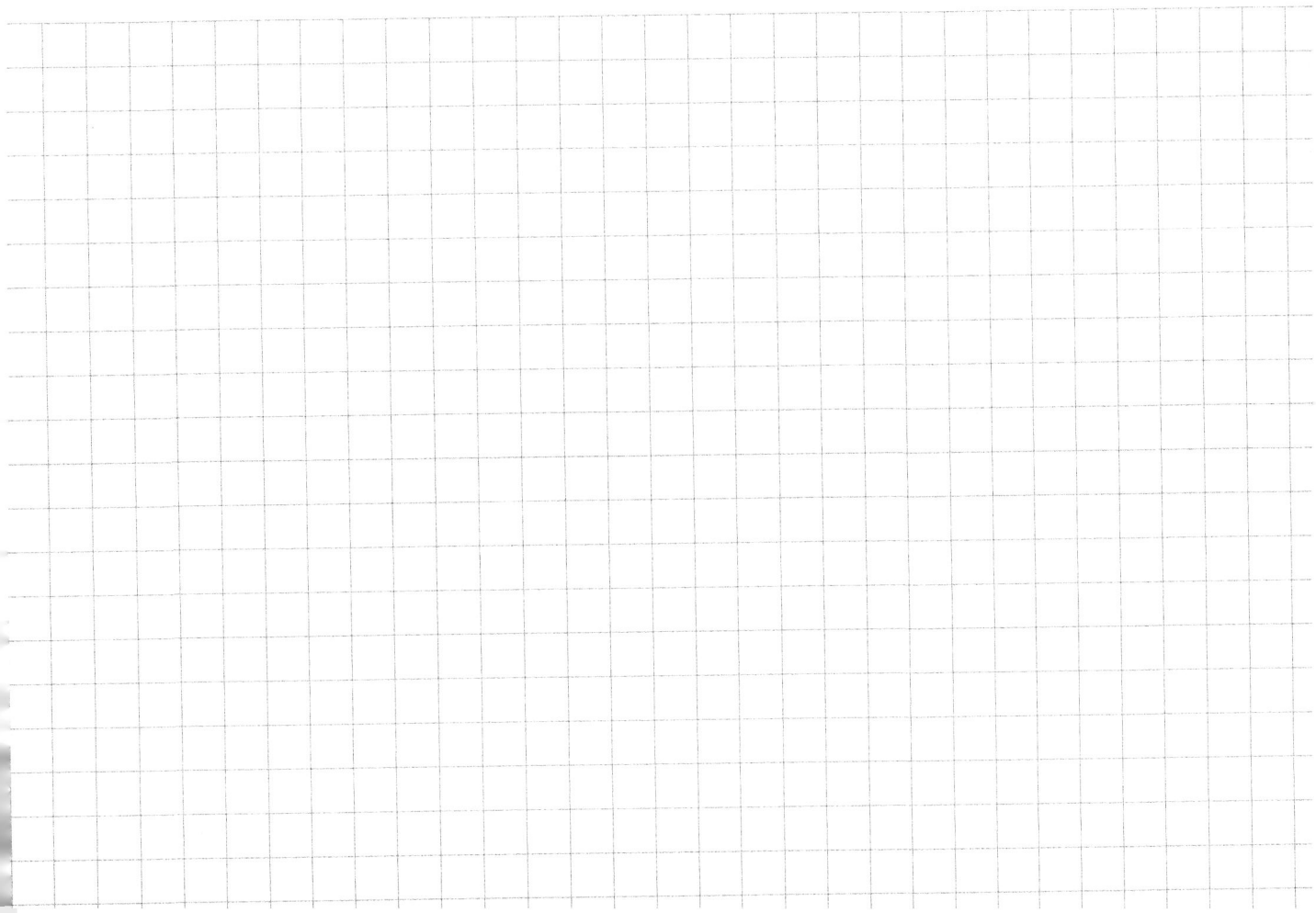

FINDER

Date	Day
Start Time	End Time
Location	
Temperature	Weather

Sketch	Directions (N S *p f*)	Intensity Estimates	Key
			0 = extremely bright 1 = bright areas 2 = general hue of disc 3 = shading near limit of visibility 4 = shading well seen 5 = unusually dark shading

Instrument	Seeing (Antoniadi Scale) I II III IV V
Magnification	Filters: W#
Sky very bright bright fair twilight dark	Transparency very good good fair poor
Phase Estimate: % filter W#	Disc Diameter
Illuminated Disc	Unilluminated Disc

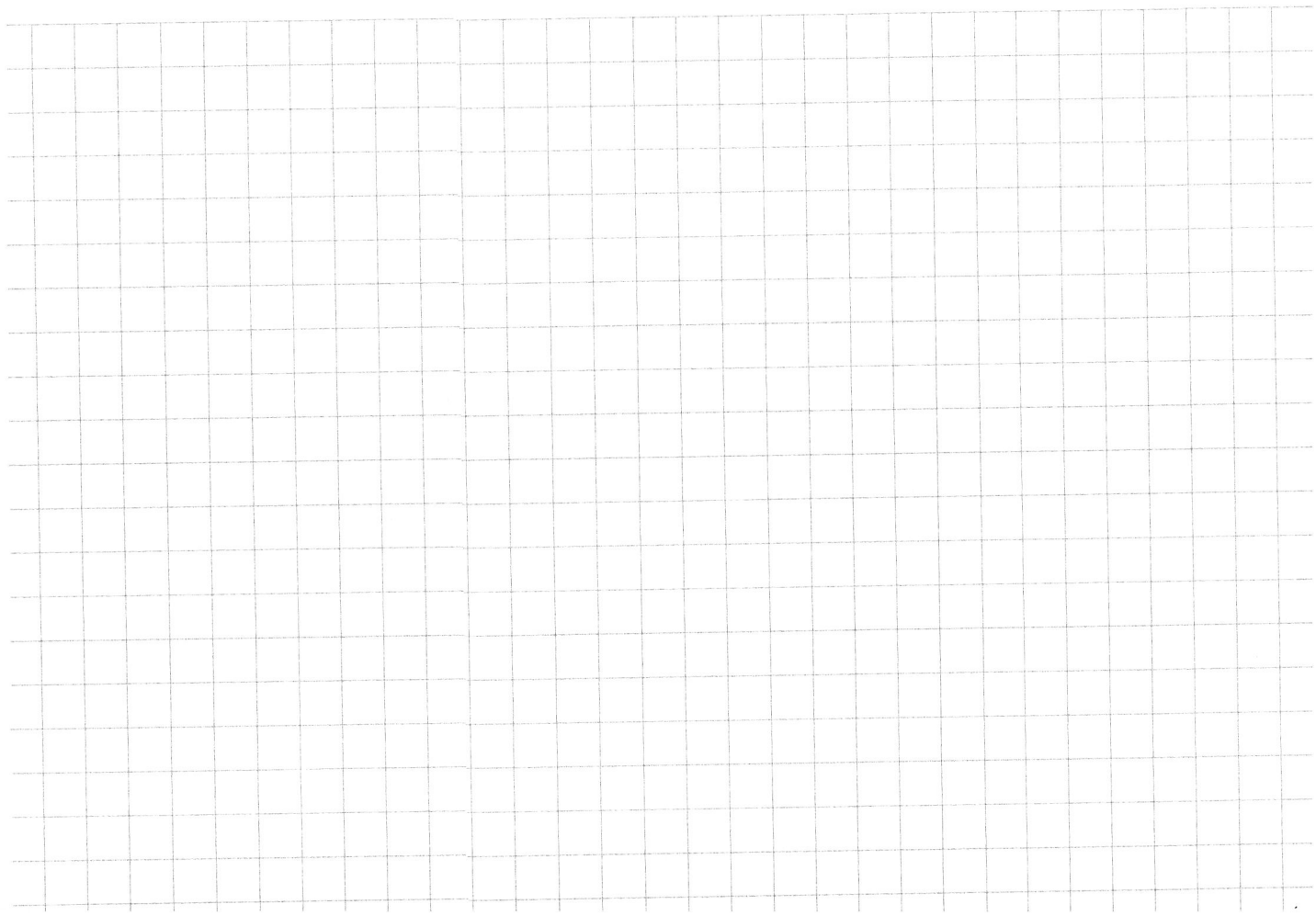

FINDER

Date		Day	
Start Time		End Time	
Location			
Temperature		Weather	

Sketch	Directions (N S p f)	Intensity Estimates	Key
	↕ ↔		0 = extremely bright 1 = bright areas 2 = general hue of disc 3 = shading near limit of visibility 4 = shading well seen 5 = unusually dark shading

Instrument	Seeing (Antoniadi Scale)
	I II III IV V
Magnification	Filters: W#
Sky very bright bright fair twilight dark	Transparency very good good fair poor
Phase Estimate: % filter W#	Disc Diameter
Illuminated Disc	Unilluminated Disc

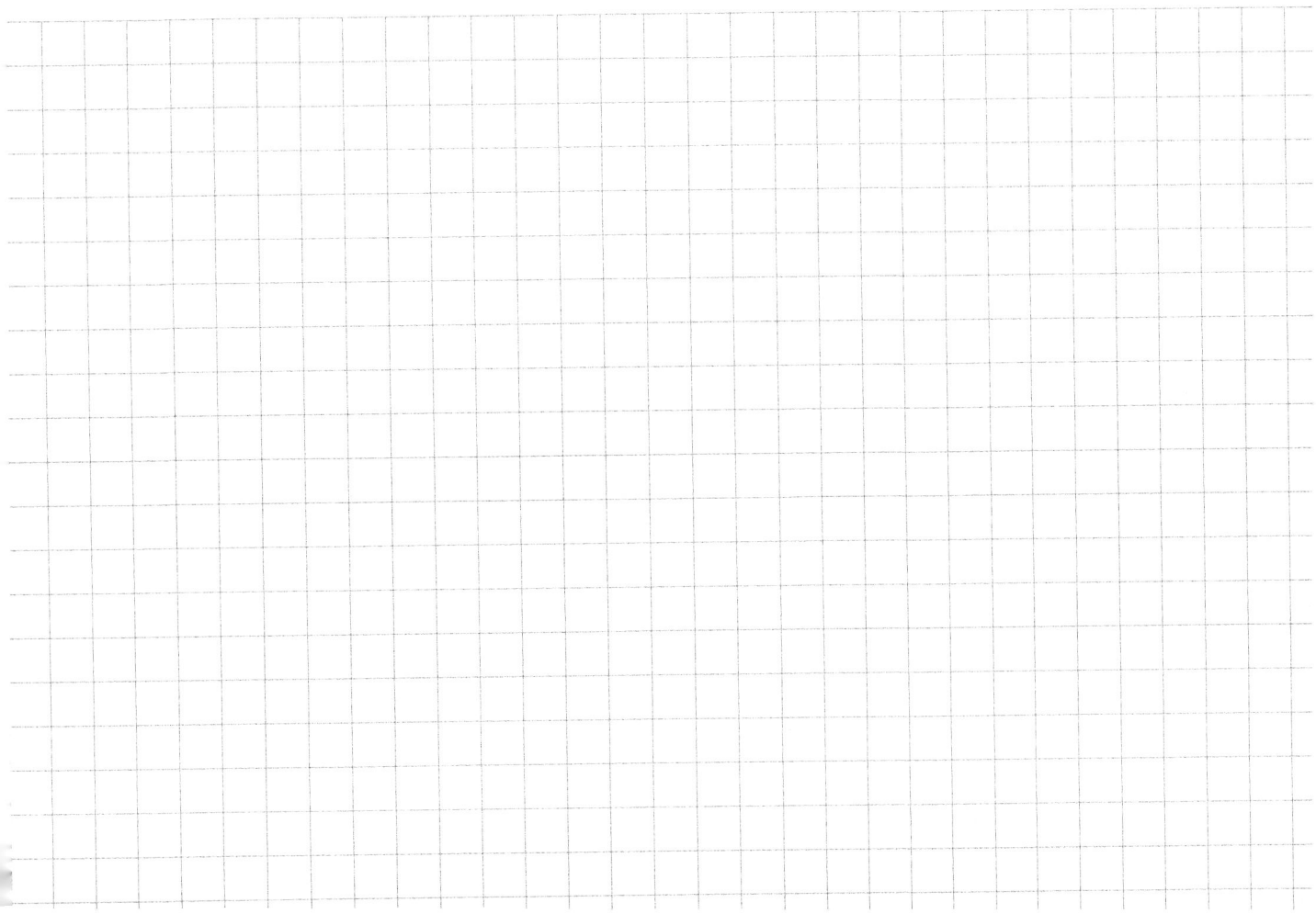

FINDER

Date	Day
Start Time	End Time
Location	
Temperature	Weather

Sketch	Directions (N S *p f*)	Intensity Estimates	Key
			0 = extremely bright 1 = bright areas 2 = general hue of disc 3 = shading near limit of visibility 4 = shading well seen 5 = unusually dark shading

Instrument	Seeing (Antoniadi Scale)
	I II III IV V
Magnification	Filters: W#
Sky very bright bright fair twilight dark	Transparency very good good fair poor
Phase Estimate: % filter W#	Disc Diameter
Illuminated Disc	Unilluminated Disc

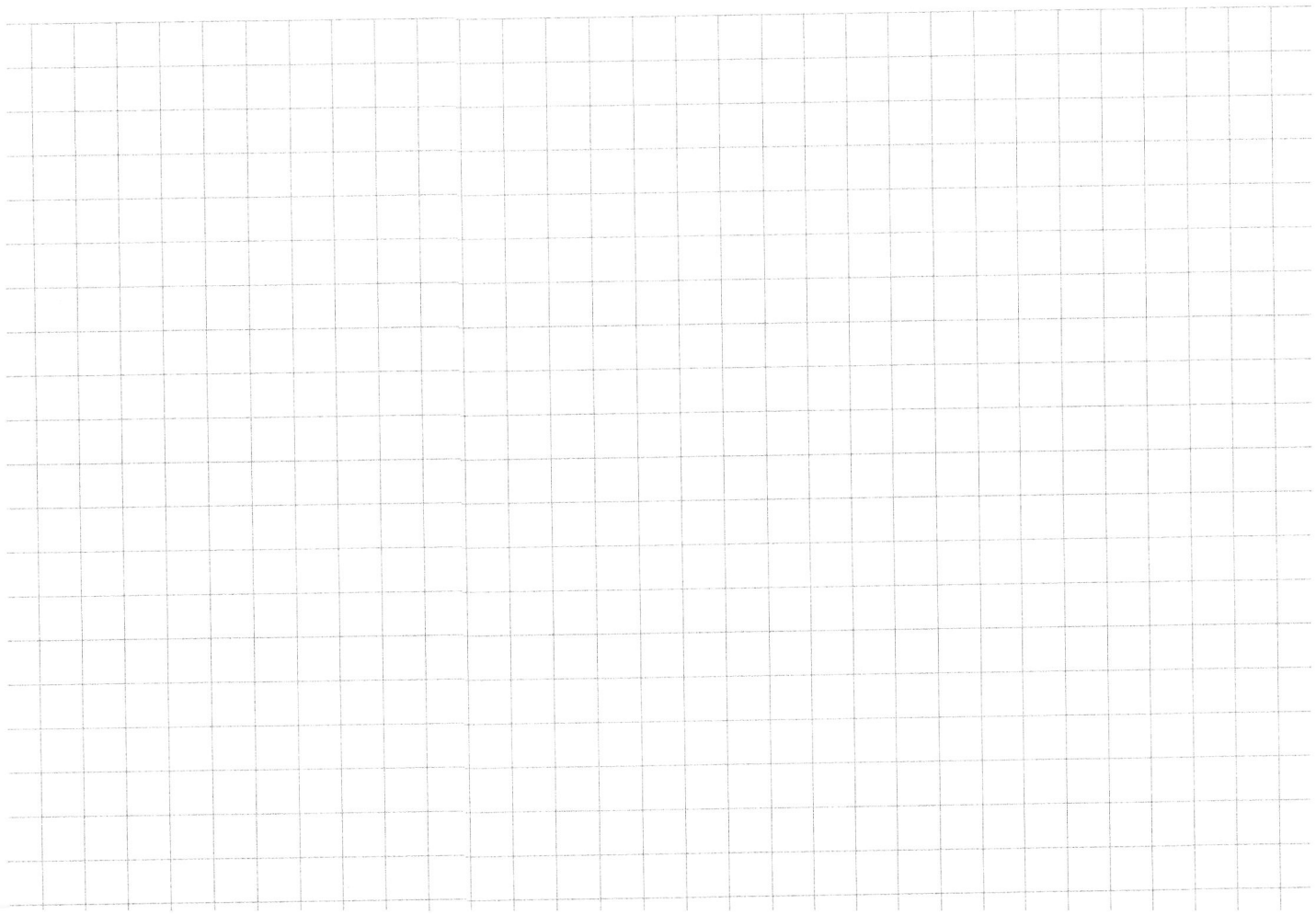

FINDER

Date		Day	
Start Time		End Time	
Location			
Temperature		Weather	

Sketch	Directions (N S *p f*)	Intensity Estimates	Key
○	↕ ↔	○	0 = extremely bright 1 = bright areas 2 = general hue of disc 3 = shading near limit of visibility 4 = shading well seen 5 = unusually dark shading

Instrument	Seeing (Antoniadi Scale)
	I II III IV V
Magnification	Filters: W#
Sky very bright bright fair twilight dark	Transparency very good good fair poor
Phase Estimate: % filter W#	Disc Diameter
Illuminated Disc	Unilluminated Disc

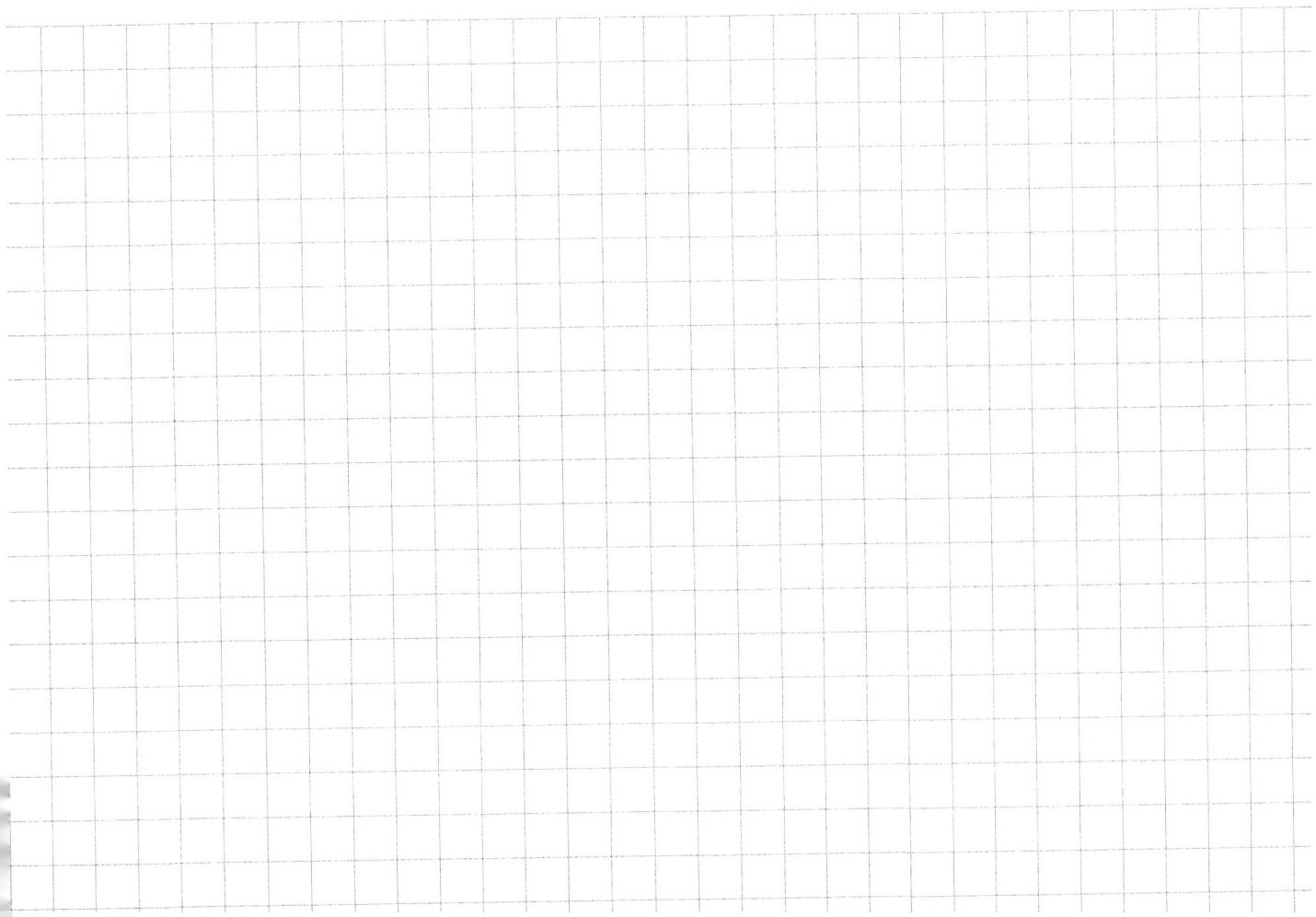

FINDER

Date		Day	
Start Time		**End Time**	
Location			
Temperature		**Weather**	

Sketch	Directions (N S *p f*)	Intensity Estimates	Key
			0 = extremely bright 1 = bright areas 2 = general hue of disc 3 = shading near limit of visibility 4 = shading well seen 5 = unusually dark shading

Instrument	Seeing (Antoniadi Scale)
	I II III IV V
Magnification	Filters: W#
Sky very bright bright fair twilight dark	Transparency very good good fair poor
Phase Estimate: % filter W#	Disc Diameter
Illuminated Disc	Unilluminated Disc

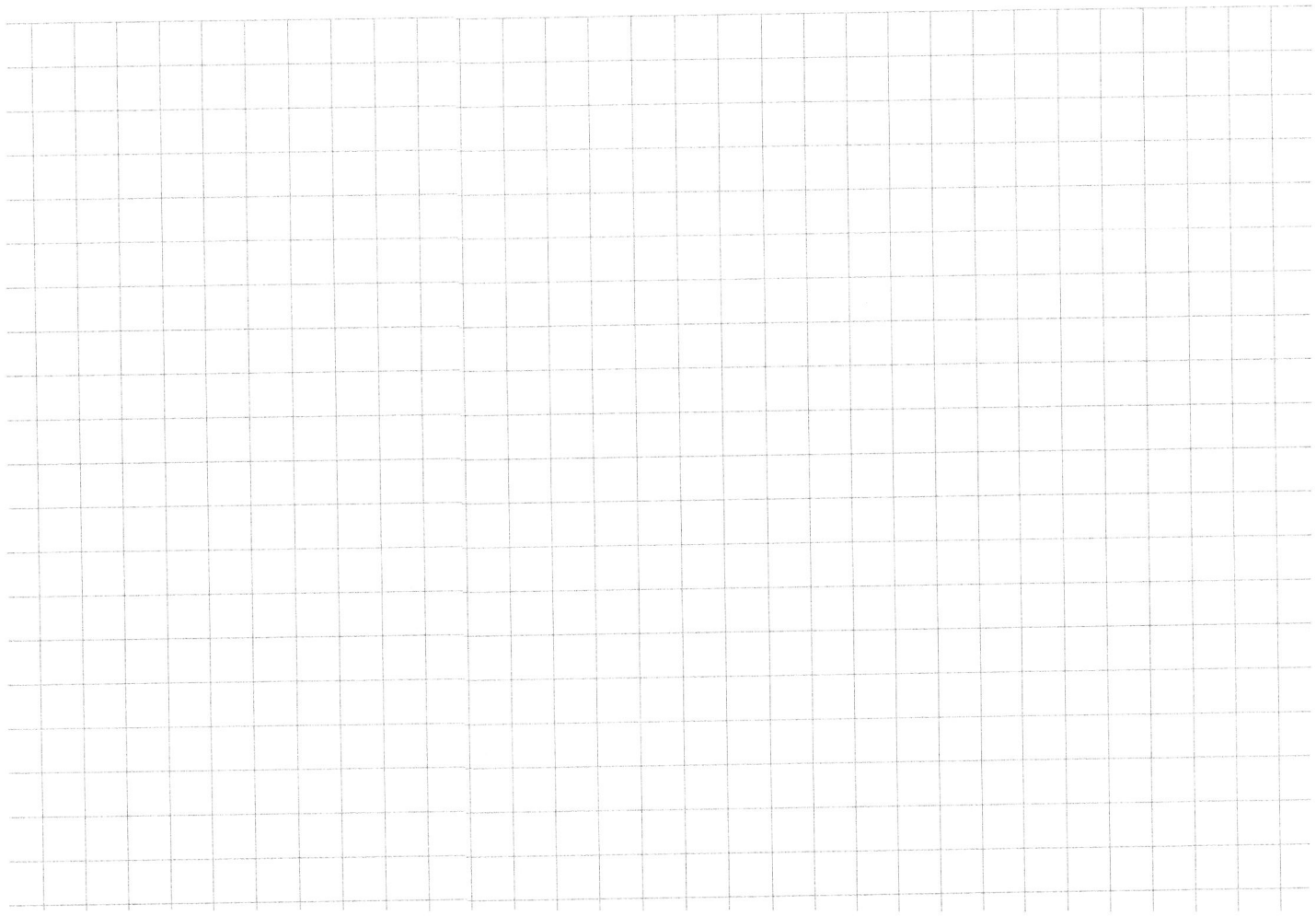

FINDER

Date		Day	
Start Time		End Time	
Location			
Temperature		Weather	

Sketch	Directions (N S *p f*)	Intensity Estimates	Key
	↕ ↔		0 = extremely bright 1 = bright areas 2 = general hue of disc 3 = shading near limit of visibility 4 = shading well seen 5 = unusually dark shading

Instrument	Seeing (Antoniadi Scale)
	I II III IV V
Magnification	Filters: W#
Sky very bright bright fair twilight dark	Transparency very good good fair poor
Phase Estimate: % filter W#	Disc Diameter
Illuminated Disc	Unilluminated Disc

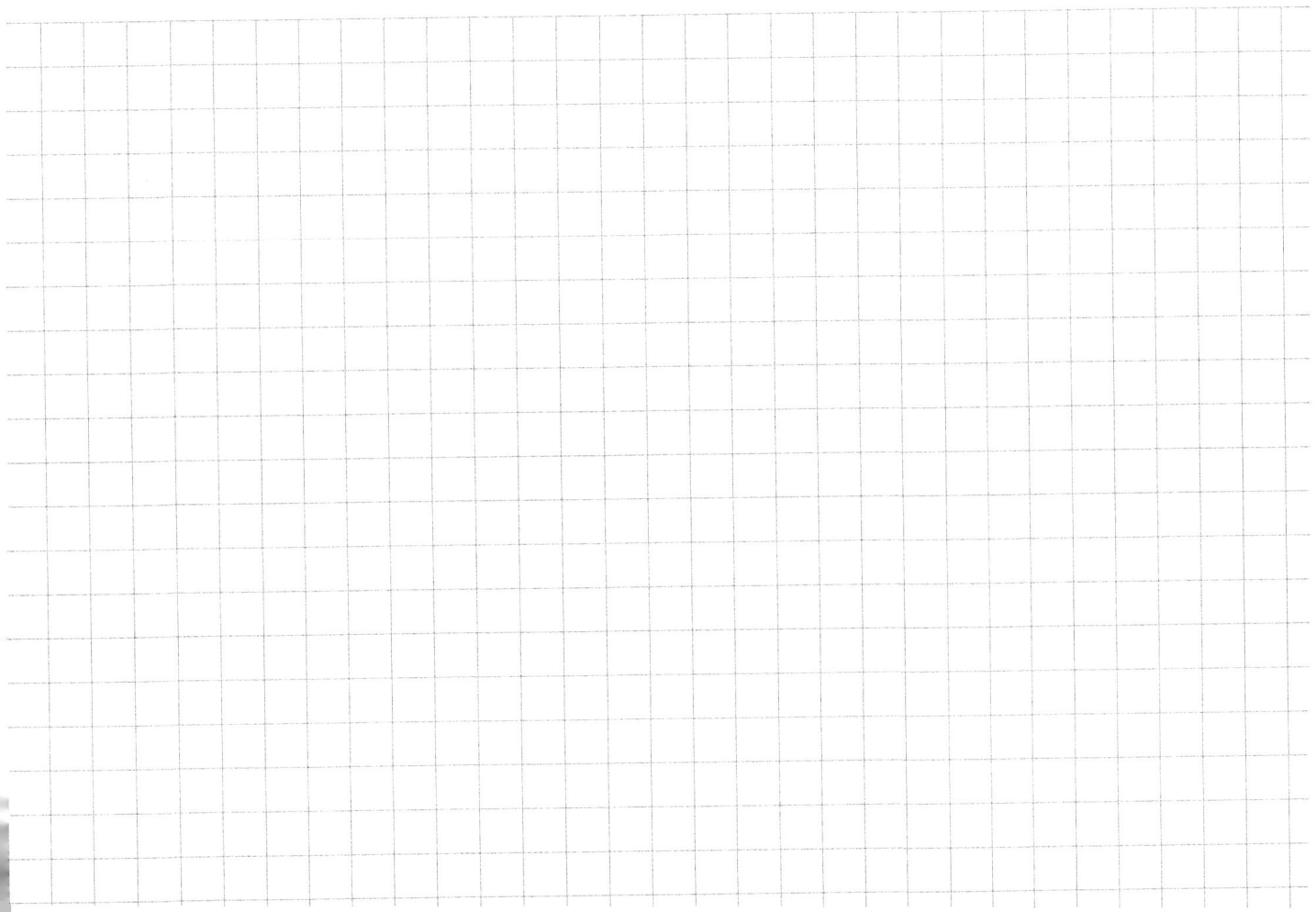

FINDER

Date	Day
Start Time	End Time
Location	
Temperature	Weather

Sketch	Directions (N S *p f*)	Intensity Estimates	Key
			0 = extremely bright 1 = bright areas 2 = general hue of disc 3 = shading near limit of visibility 4 = shading well seen 5 = unusually dark shading

Instrument	Seeing (Antoniadi Scale)
	I II III IV V
Magnification	Filters: W#
Sky very bright bright fair twilight dark	Transparency very good good fair poor
Phase Estimate: % filter W#	Disc Diameter
Illuminated Disc	Unilluminated Disc

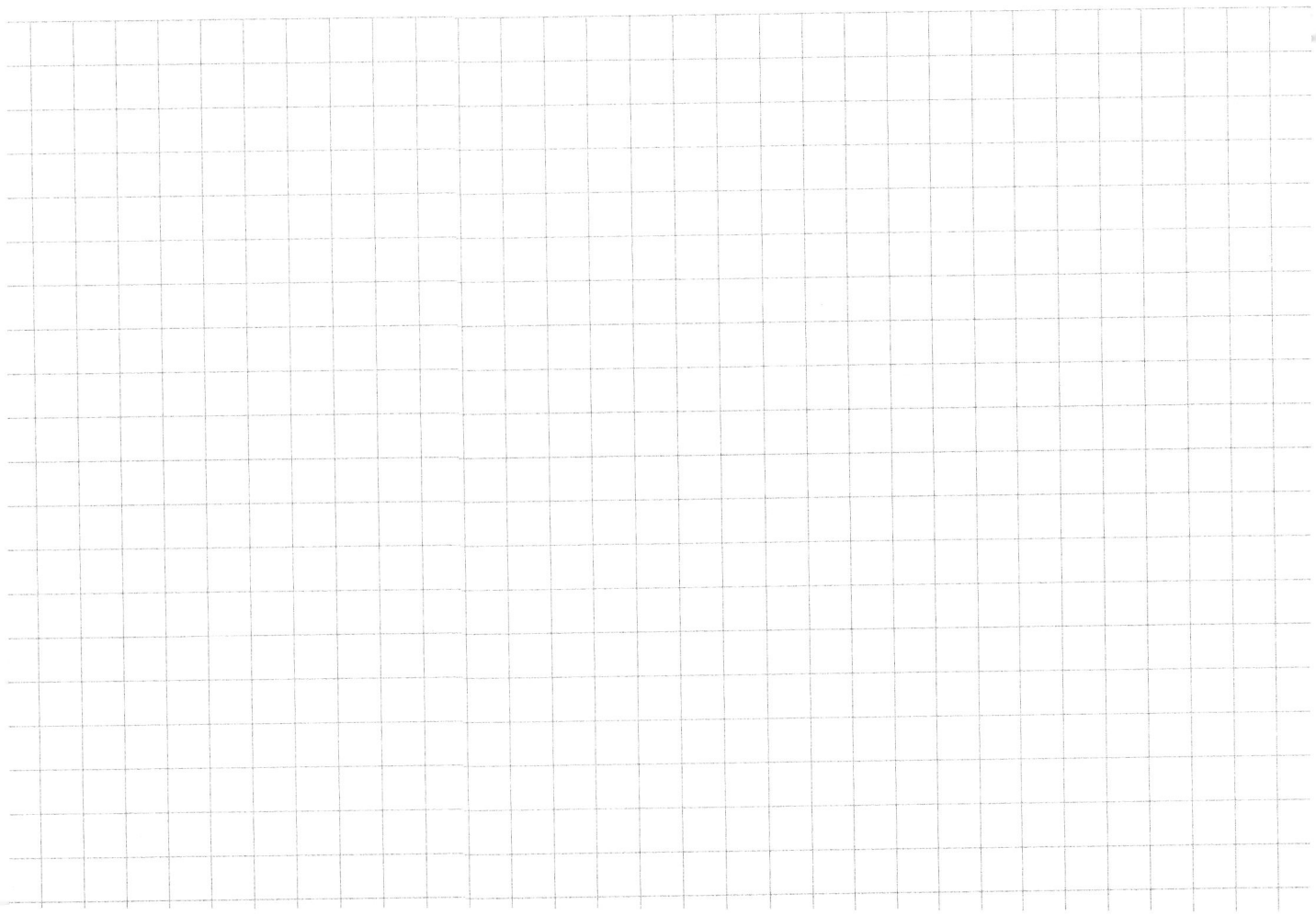

FINDER

Date	Day
Start Time	End Time
Location	
Temperature	Weather

Sketch	Directions (N S *p f*)	Intensity Estimates	Key
	↕ ↔		0 = extremely bright 1 = bright areas 2 = general hue of disc 3 = shading near limit of visibility 4 = shading well seen 5 = unusually dark shading

Instrument	Seeing (Antoniadi Scale) I II III IV V
Magnification	Filters: W#
Sky very bright bright fair twilight dark	Transparency very good good fair poor
Phase Estimate: % filter W#	Disc Diameter
Illuminated Disc	Unilluminated Disc

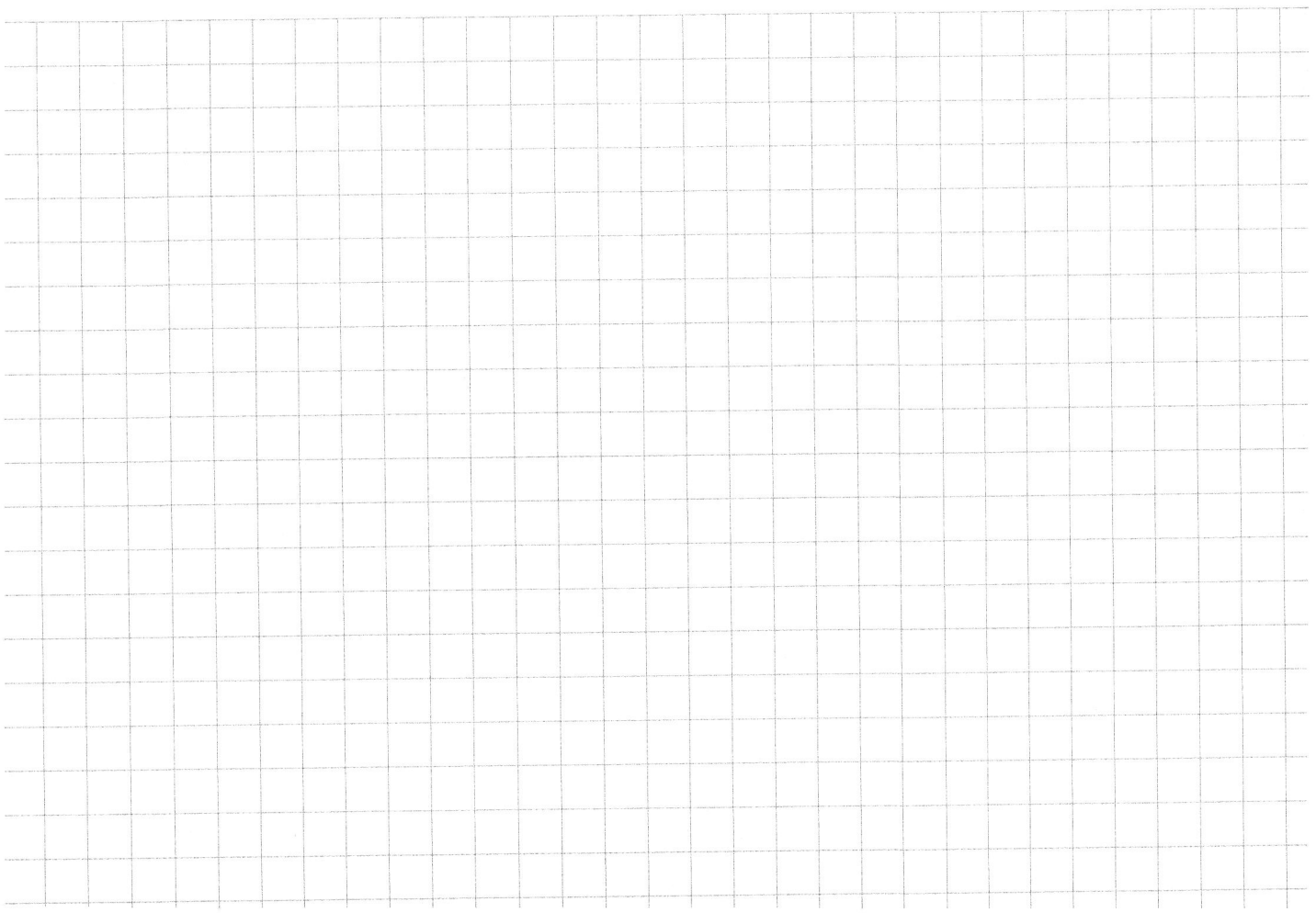

FINDER

Date	Day
Start Time	End Time
Location	
Temperature	Weather

Sketch	Directions (N S *p f*)	Intensity Estimates	Key
	↕ ↔		0 = extremely bright 1 = bright areas 2 = general hue of disc 3 = shading near limit of visibility 4 = shading well seen 5 = unusually dark shading

Instrument	Seeing (Antoniadi Scale) I II III IV V
Magnification	Filters: W#
Sky very bright bright fair twilight dark	Transparency very good good fair poor
Phase Estimate: % filter W#	Disc Diameter
Illuminated Disc	Unilluminated Disc

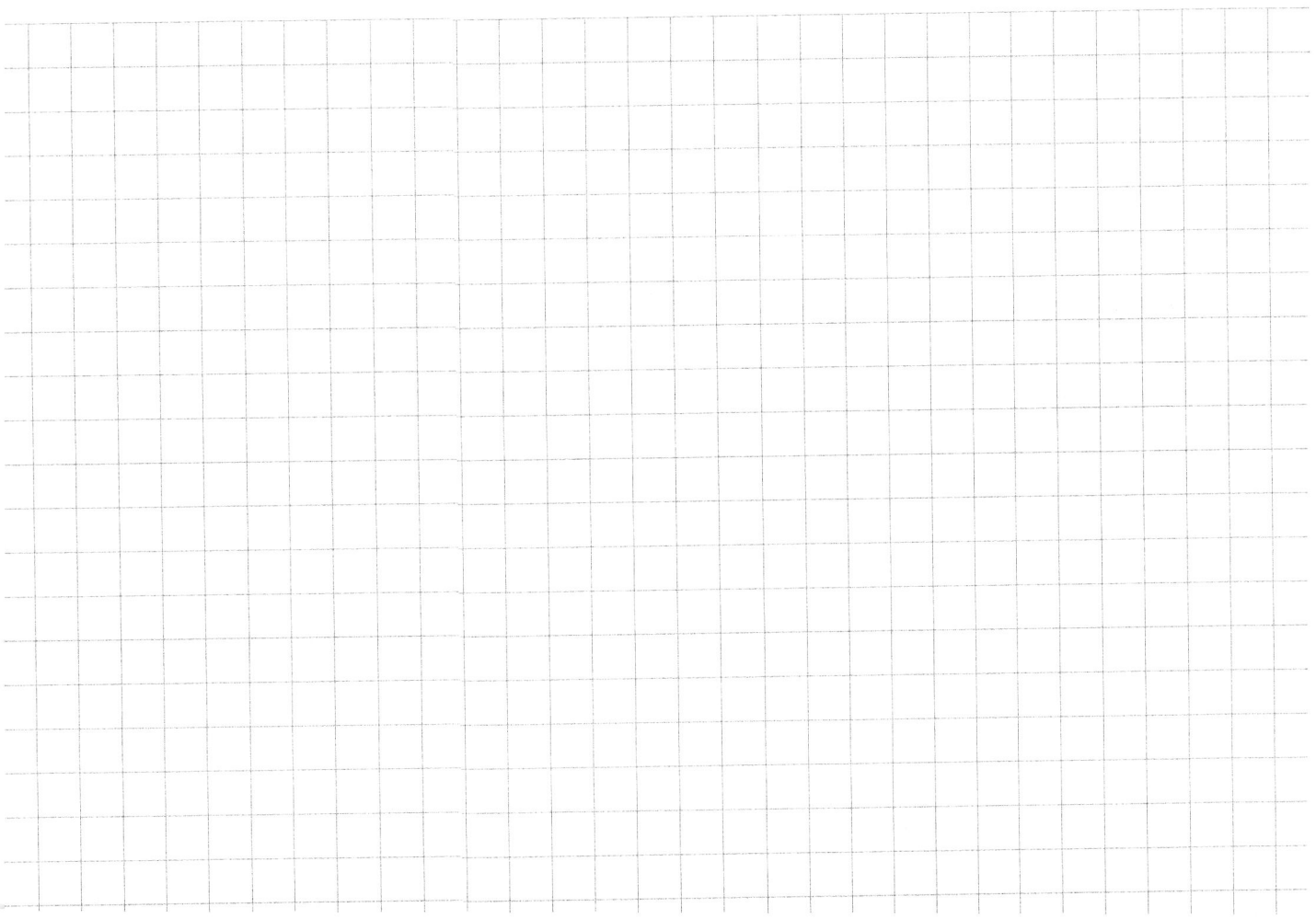

FINDER

Date		Day	
Start Time		End Time	
Location			
Temperature		Weather	

Sketch	Directions (N S p f)	Intensity Estimates	Key
	↕ ↔		0 = extremely bright 1 = bright areas 2 = general hue of disc 3 = shading near limit of visibility 4 = shading well seen 5 = unusually dark shading

Instrument	Seeing (Antoniadi Scale) I II III IV V
Magnification	Filters: W#
Sky very bright bright fair twilight dark	Transparency very good good fair poor
Phase Estimate: % filter W#	Disc Diameter
Illuminated Disc	Unilluminated Disc

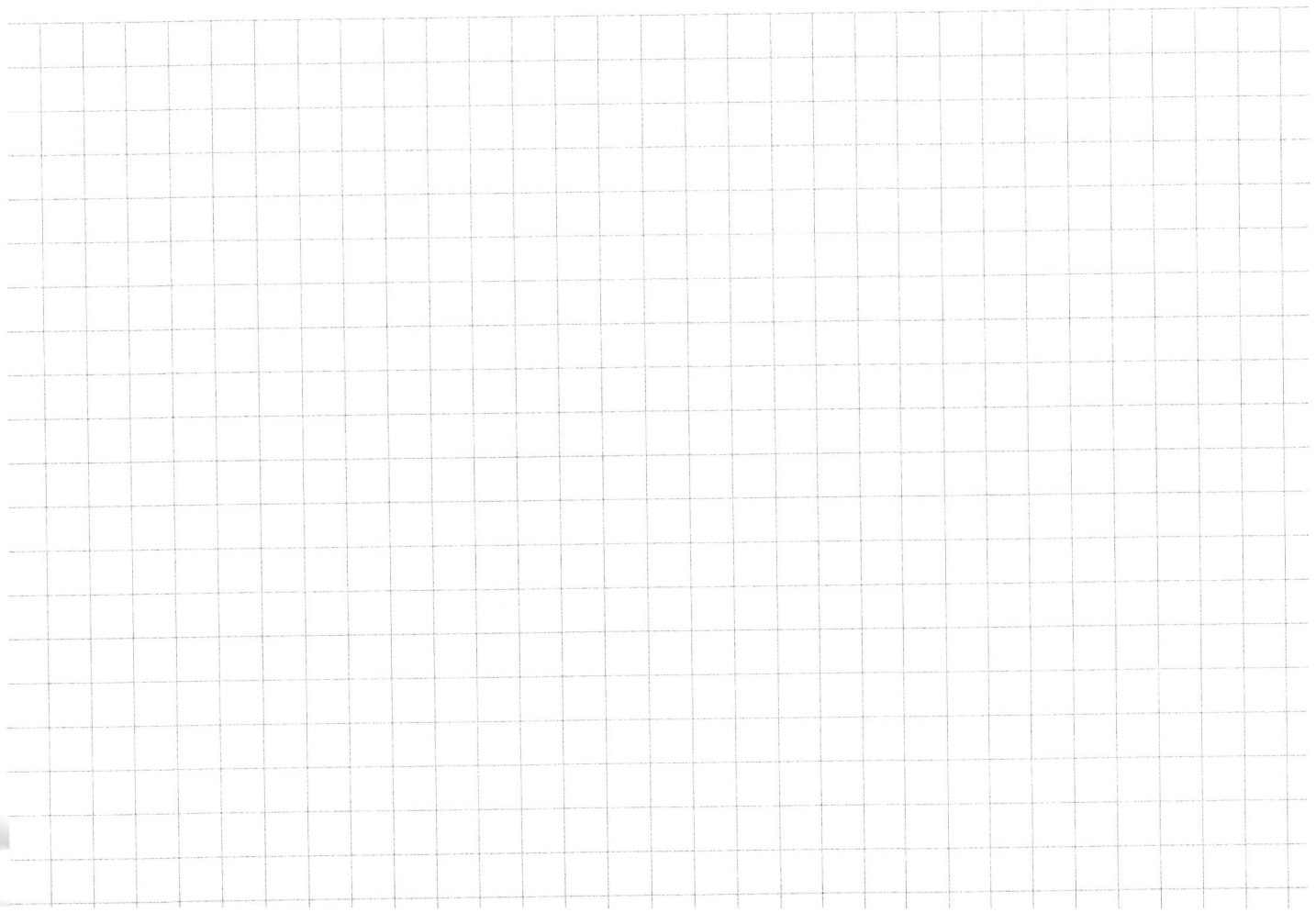

FINDER

Date	Day
Start Time	End Time
Location	
Temperature	Weather

Sketch	Directions (N S *p f*)	Intensity Estimates	Key
(circle)	↕ ↔	(circle)	0 = extremely bright 1 = bright areas 2 = general hue of disc 3 = shading near limit of visibility 4 = shading well seen 5 = unusually dark shading

Instrument	Seeing (Antoniadi Scale)
	I II III IV V
Magnification	Filters: W#
Sky very bright bright fair twilight dark	Transparency very good good fair poor
Phase Estimate: % filter W#	Disc Diameter
Illuminated Disc	Unilluminated Disc

FINDER

Date		Day	
Start Time		End Time	
Location			
Temperature		Weather	

Sketch	Directions (N S *p f*)	Intensity Estimates	Key
	↕ ↔		0 = extremely bright 1 = bright areas 2 = general hue of disc 3 = shading near limit of visibility 4 = shading well seen 5 = unusually dark shading

Instrument	Seeing (Antoniadi Scale)
	I II III IV V
Magnification	Filters: W#
Sky very bright bright fair twilight dark	Transparency very good good fair poor
Phase Estimate: % filter W#	Disc Diameter
Illuminated Disc	Unilluminated Disc

FINDER

Date	Day
Start Time	End Time
Location	
Temperature	Weather

Sketch	Directions (N S p f)	Intensity Estimates	Key
	↕ ↔		0 = extremely bright 1 = bright areas 2 = general hue of disc 3 = shading near limit of visibility 4 = shading well seen 5 = unusually dark shading

Instrument	Seeing (Antoniadi Scale) I II III IV V
Magnification	Filters: W#
Sky very bright bright fair twilight dark	Transparency very good good fair poor
Phase Estimate: % filter W#	Disc Diameter
Illuminated Disc	Unilluminated Disc

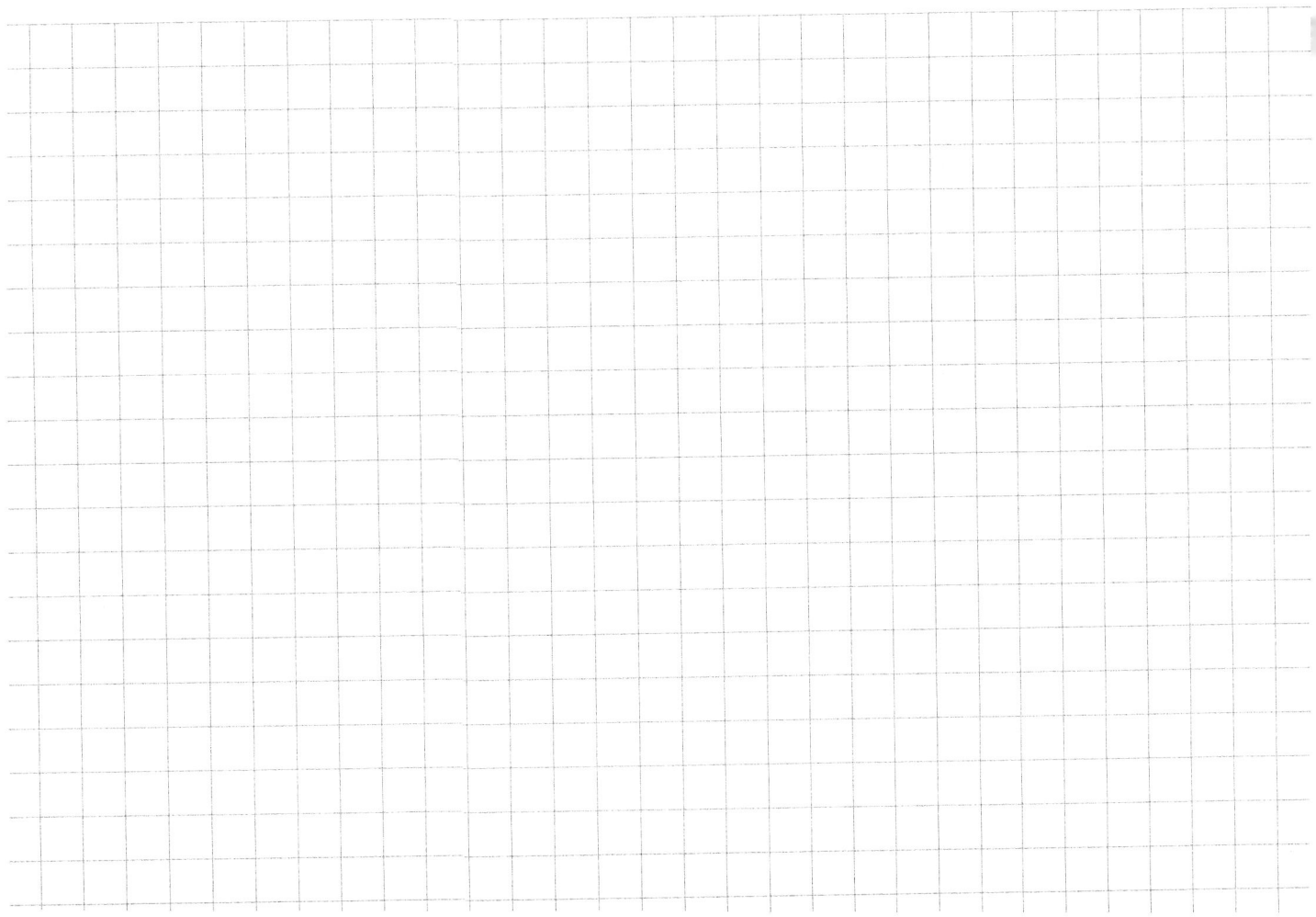

FINDER

Date	Day
Start Time	End Time
Location	
Temperature	Weather

Sketch	Directions (N S p f)	Intensity Estimates	Key
			0 = extremely bright 1 = bright areas 2 = general hue of disc 3 = shading near limit of visibility 4 = shading well seen 5 = unusually dark shading

Instrument	Seeing (Antoniadi Scale)
	I II III IV V
Magnification	Filters: W#
Sky very bright bright fair twilight dark	Transparency very good good fair poor
Phase Estimate: % filter W#	Disc Diameter
Illuminated Disc	Unilluminated Disc

FINDER

Date		Day	
Start Time		End Time	
Location			
Temperature		Weather	

Sketch	Directions (N S *p f*)	Intensity Estimates	Key
			0 = extremely bright 1 = bright areas 2 = general hue of disc 3 = shading near limit of visibility 4 = shading well seen 5 = unusually dark shading

Instrument	Seeing (Antoniadi Scale)
	I II III IV V
Magnification	Filters: W#
Sky very bright bright fair twilight dark	Transparency very good good fair poor
Phase Estimate: % filter W#	Disc Diameter
Illuminated Disc	Unilluminated Disc

FINDER

Date		Day	
Start Time		**End Time**	
Location			
Temperature		Weather	

Sketch	Directions (N S *p f*)	Intensity Estimates	Key
	↕ ↔		0 = extremely bright 1 = bright areas 2 = general hue of disc 3 = shading near limit of visibility 4 = shading well seen 5 = unusually dark shading

Instrument	Seeing (Antoniadi Scale)
	I II III IV V
Magnification	Filters: W#
Sky very bright bright fair twilight dark	Transparency very good good fair poor
Phase Estimate: % filter W#	Disc Diameter
Illuminated Disc	Unilluminated Disc

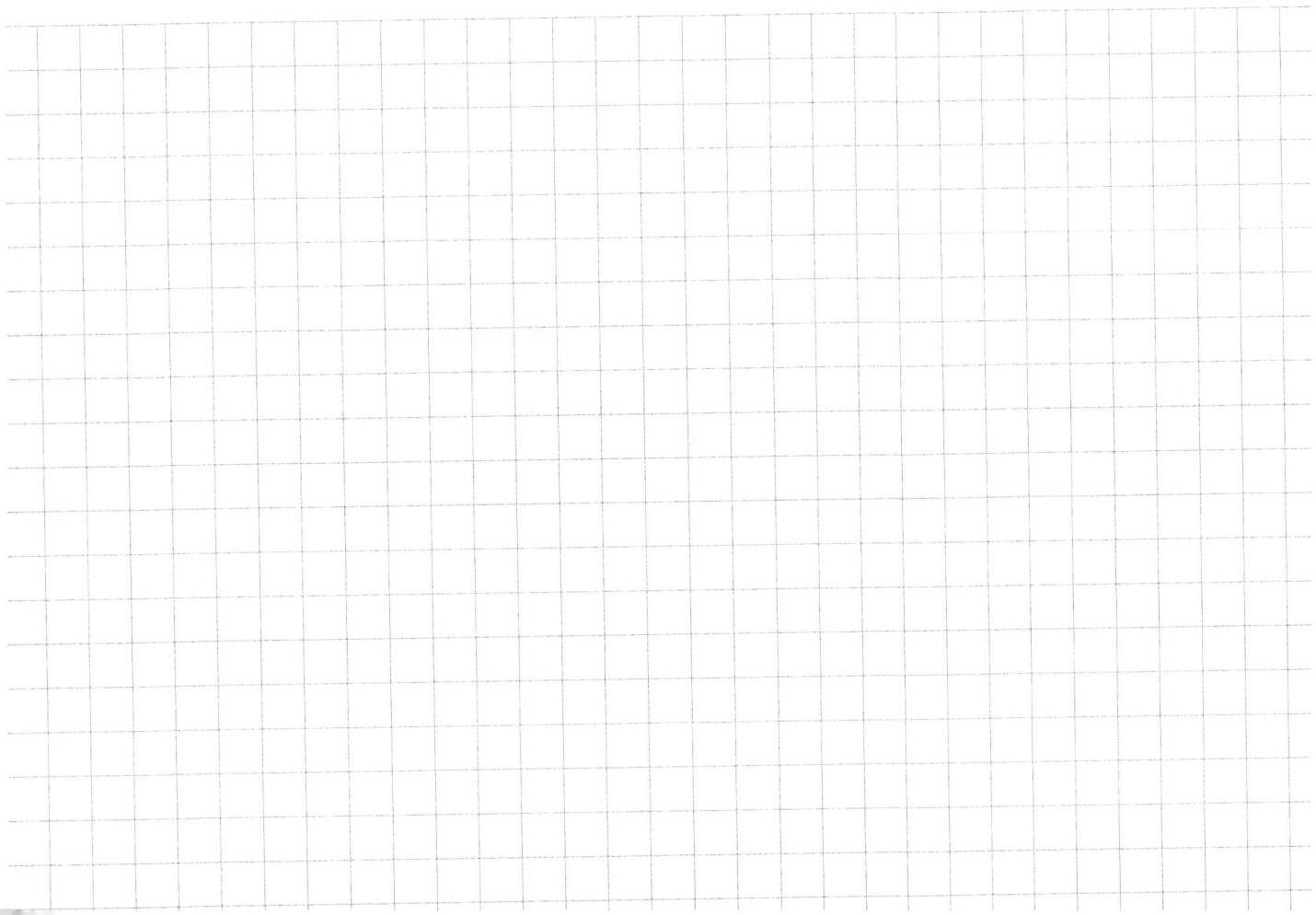

FINDER

Date	Day
Start Time	End Time
Location	
Temperature	Weather

Sketch	Directions (N S *p f*)	Intensity Estimates	Key
○	↕ ↔	○	0 = extremely bright 1 = bright areas 2 = general hue of disc 3 = shading near limit of visibility 4 = shading well seen 5 = unusually dark shading

Instrument	Seeing (Antoniadi Scale) I II III IV V
Magnification	Filters: W#
Sky very bright bright fair twilight dark	Transparency very good good fair poor
Phase Estimate: % filter W#	Disc Diameter
Illuminated Disc	Unilluminated Disc

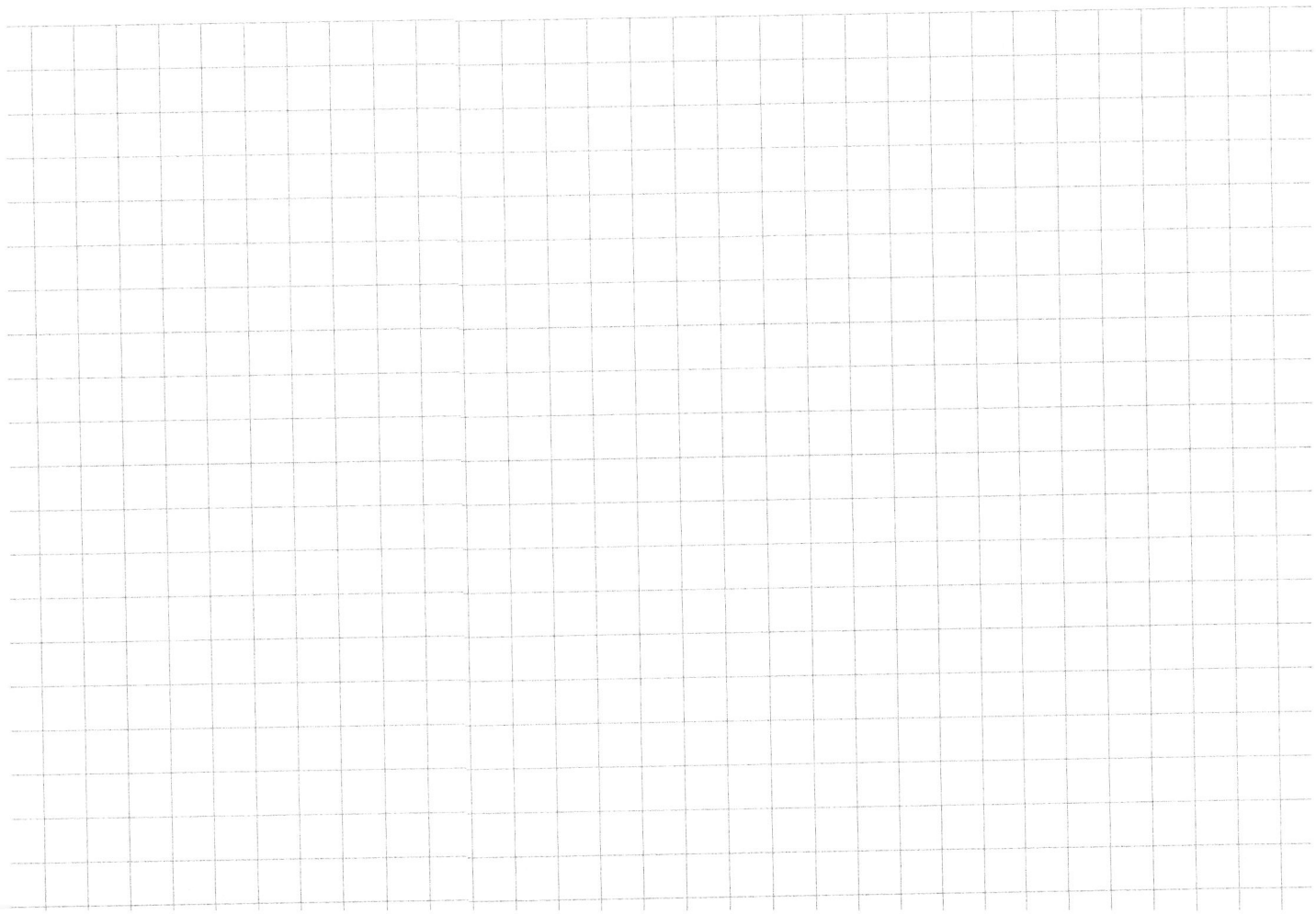

FINDER

Date	Day
Start Time	End Time
Location	
Temperature	Weather

Sketch	Directions (N S *p f*)	Intensity Estimates	Key
	↕ ↔		0 = extremely bright 1 = bright areas 2 = general hue of disc 3 = shading near limit of visibility 4 = shading well seen 5 = unusually dark shading

Instrument	Seeing (Antoniadi Scale) I II III IV V
Magnification	Filters: W#
Sky very bright bright fair twilight dark	Transparency very good good fair poor
Phase Estimate: % filter W#	Disc Diameter
Illuminated Disc	Unilluminated Disc

FINDER

Date	Day
Start Time	End Time
Location	
Temperature	Weather

Sketch	Directions (N S p f)	Intensity Estimates	Key
	↕ ↔		0 = extremely bright 1 = bright areas 2 = general hue of disc 3 = shading near limit of visibility 4 = shading well seen 5 = unusually dark shading

Instrument	Seeing (Antoniadi Scale)
	I II III IV V
Magnification	Filters: W#
Sky very bright bright fair twilight dark	Transparency very good good fair poor
Phase Estimate: % filter W#	Disc Diameter
Illuminated Disc	Unilluminated Disc

FINDER

Date	Day
Start Time	End Time
Location	
Temperature	Weather

Sketch	Directions (N S p f)	Intensity Estimates	Key
			0 = extremely bright 1 = bright areas 2 = general hue of disc 3 = shading near limit of visibility 4 = shading well seen 5 = unusually dark shading

Instrument	Seeing (Antoniadi Scale) I II III IV V
Magnification	Filters: W#
Sky very bright bright fair twilight dark	Transparency very good good fair poor
Phase Estimate: % filter W#	Disc Diameter
Illuminated Disc	Unilluminated Disc

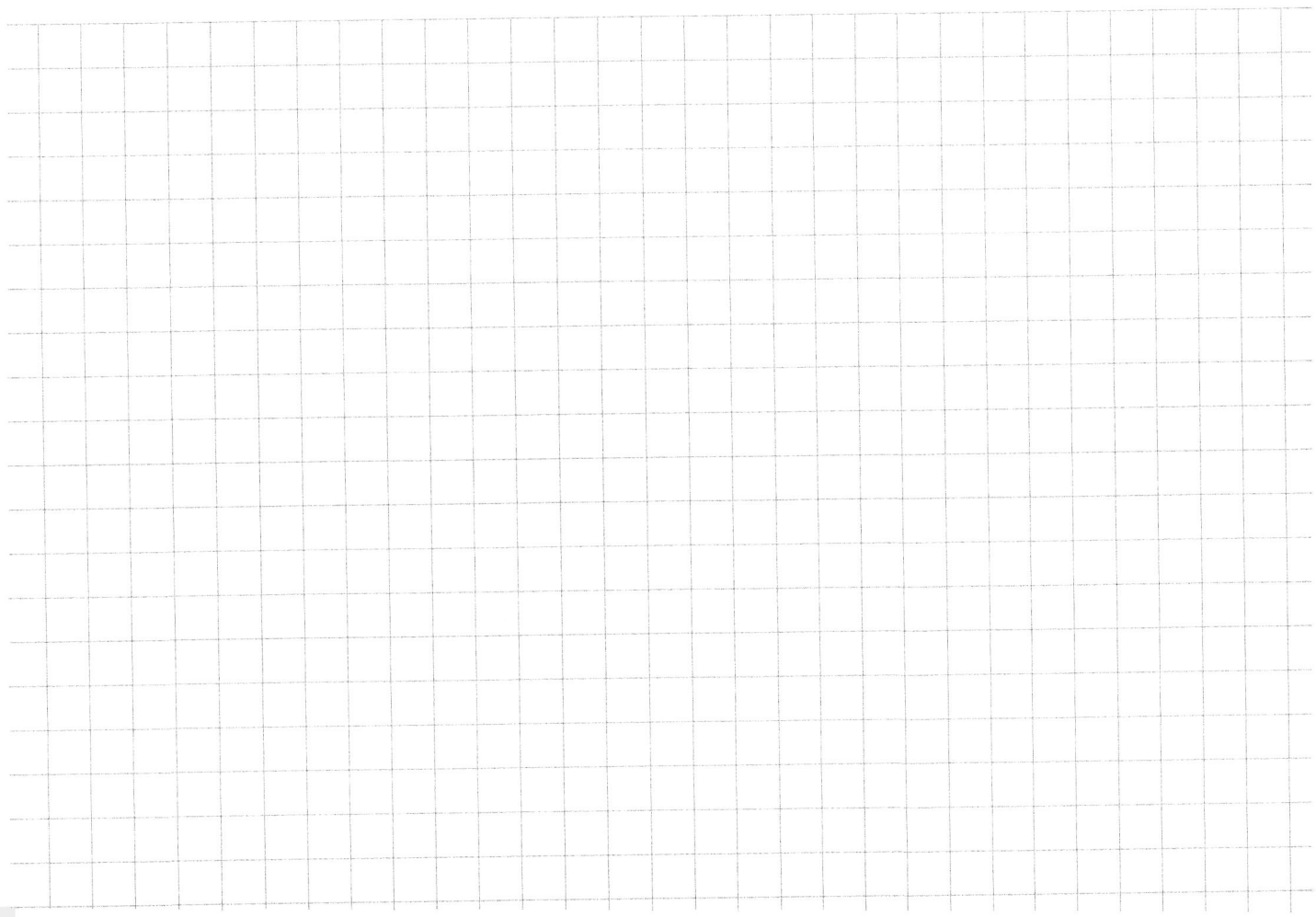

FINDER

Date		Day	
Start Time		End Time	
Location			
Temperature		Weather	

Sketch	Directions (N S p f)	Intensity Estimates	Key
◯	↕ ↔	◯	0 = extremely bright 1 = bright areas 2 = general hue of disc 3 = shading near limit of visibility 4 = shading well seen 5 = unusually dark shading

Instrument	Seeing (Antoniadi Scale)
	I II III IV V
Magnification	Filters: W#
Sky very bright bright fair twilight dark	Transparency very good good fair poor
Phase Estimate: % filter W#	Disc Diameter
Illuminated Disc	Unilluminated Disc

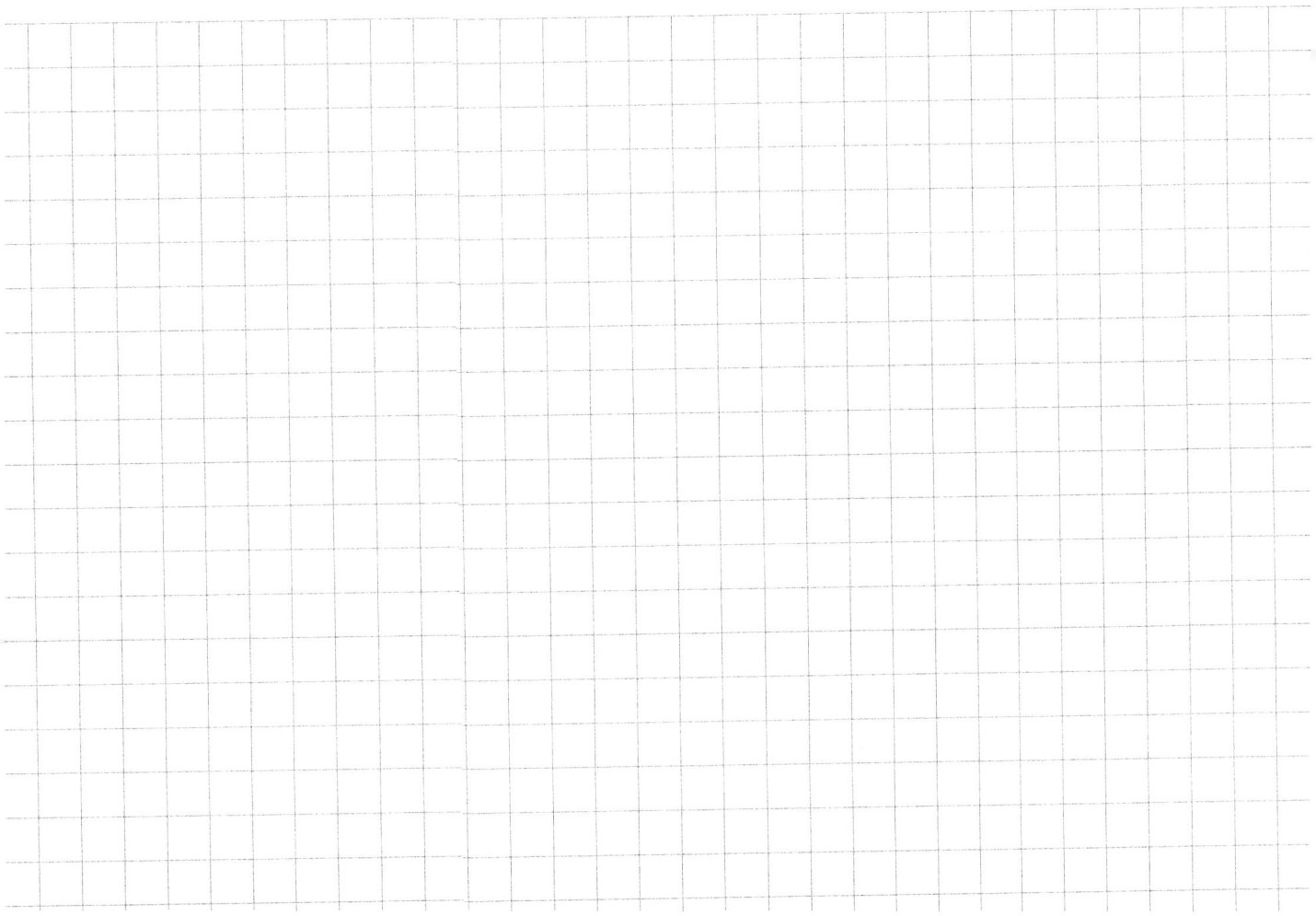

FINDER

Date	Day
Start Time	End Time
Location	
Temperature	Weather

Sketch	Directions (N S *p f*)	Intensity Estimates	Key
	↕ ↔		0 = extremely bright 1 = bright areas 2 = general hue of disc 3 = shading near limit of visibility 4 = shading well seen 5 = unusually dark shading

Instrument	Seeing (Antoniadi Scale)
	I II III IV V
Magnification	Filters: W#
Sky very bright bright fair twilight dark	Transparency very good good fair poor
Phase Estimate: % filter W#	Disc Diameter
Illuminated Disc	Unilluminated Disc

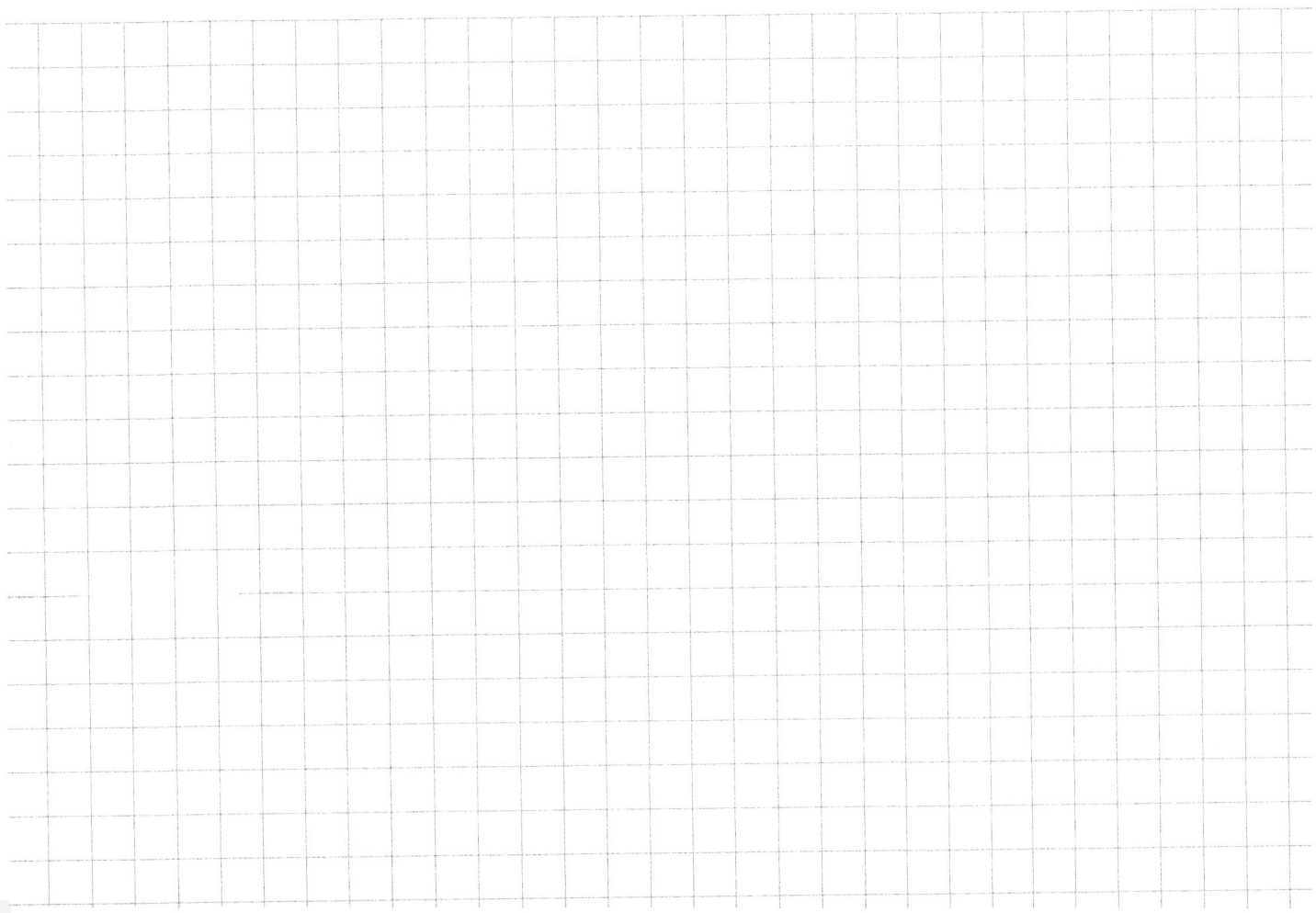

FINDER

Date	Day
Start Time	End Time
Location	
Temperature	Weather

Sketch	Directions (N S *p f*)	Intensity Estimates	Key
(circle)	↕ ↔	(circle)	0 = extremely bright 1 = bright areas 2 = general hue of disc 3 = shading near limit of visibility 4 = shading well seen 5 = unusually dark shading

Instrument	Seeing (Antoniadi Scale) I II III IV V
Magnification	Filters: W#
Sky very bright bright fair twilight dark	Transparency very good good fair poor
Phase Estimate: % filter W#	Disc Diameter
Illuminated Disc	Unilluminated Disc

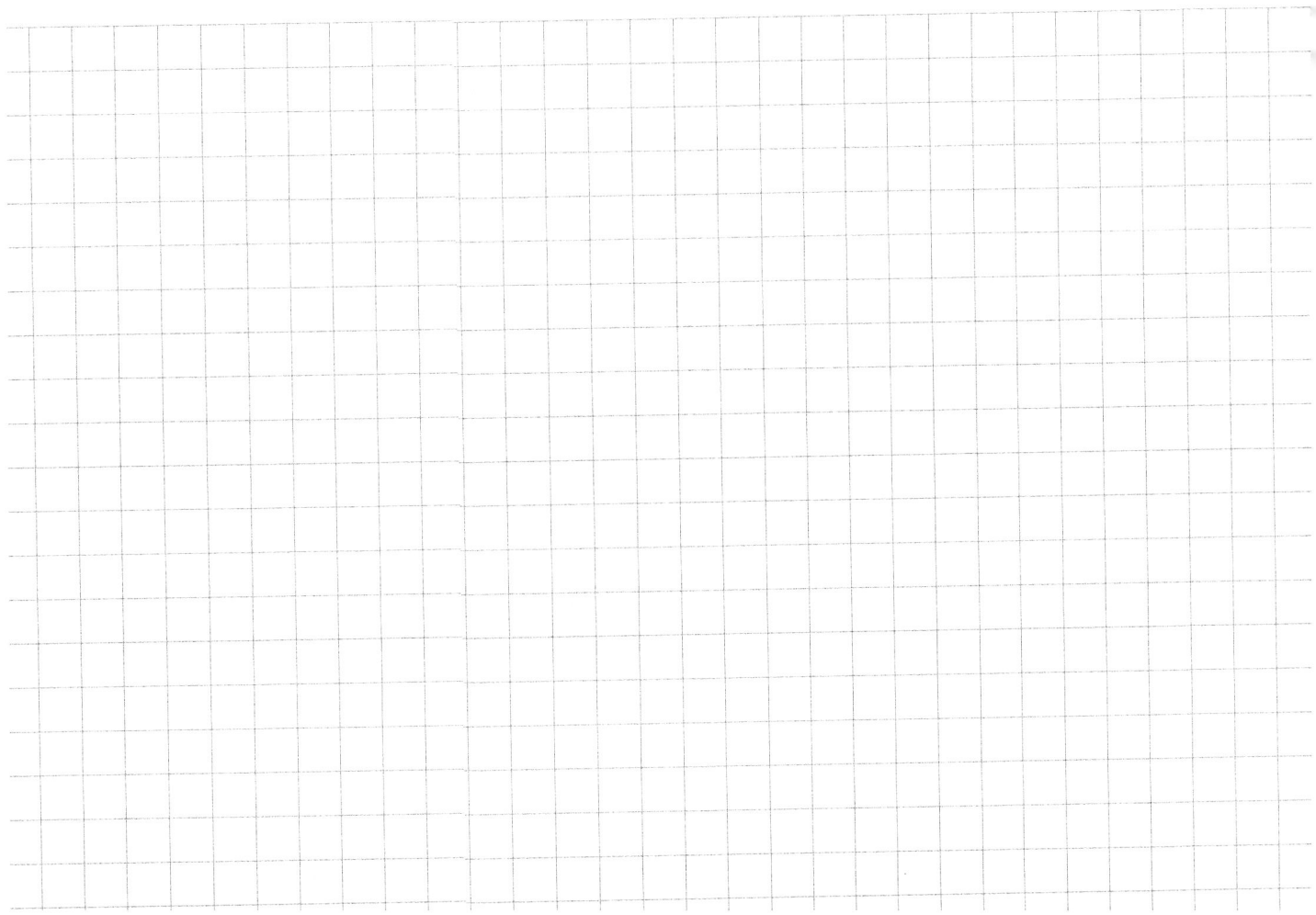

FINDER

Date	Day
Start Time	End Time
Location	
Temperature	Weather

Sketch	Directions (N S *p f*)	Intensity Estimates	Key
	↕ ↔		0 = extremely bright 1 = bright areas 2 = general hue of disc 3 = shading near limit of visibility 4 = shading well seen 5 = unusually dark shading

Instrument	Seeing (Antoniadi Scale) I II III IV V
Magnification	Filters: W#
Sky very bright bright fair twilight dark	Transparency very good good fair poor
Phase Estimate: % filter W#	Disc Diameter
Illuminated Disc	Unilluminated Disc

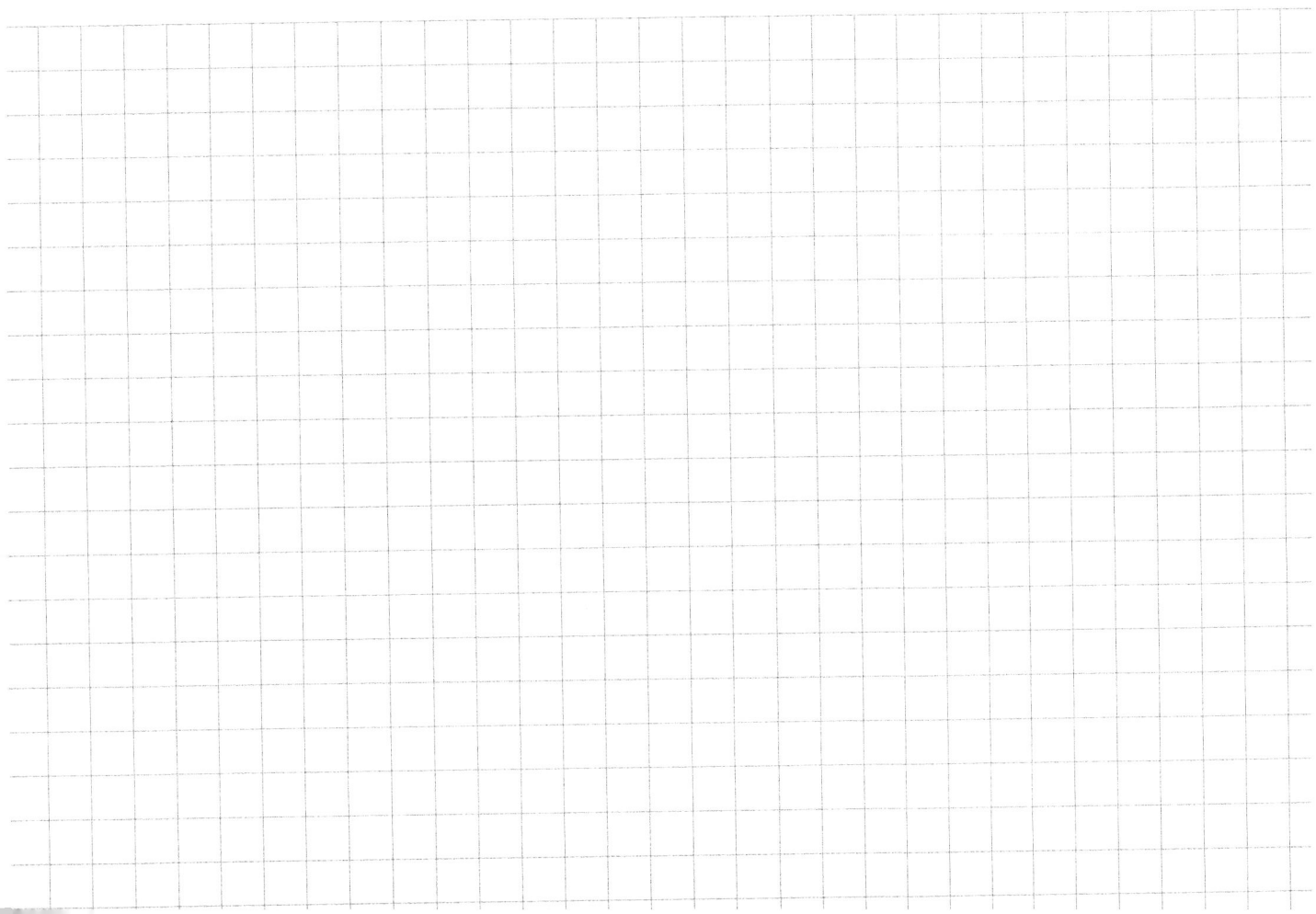

FINDER

Date		Day	
Start Time		End Time	
Location			
Temperature		Weather	

Sketch	Directions (N S p f)	Intensity Estimates	Key
	↕ ↔		0 = extremely bright 1 = bright areas 2 = general hue of disc 3 = shading near limit of visibility 4 = shading well seen 5 = unusually dark shading

Instrument	Seeing (Antoniadi Scale)
	I II III IV V
Magnification	Filters: W#
Sky	Transparency
very bright bright fair twilight dark	very good good fair poor
Phase Estimate: % filter W#	Disc Diameter
Illuminated Disc	Unilluminated Disc

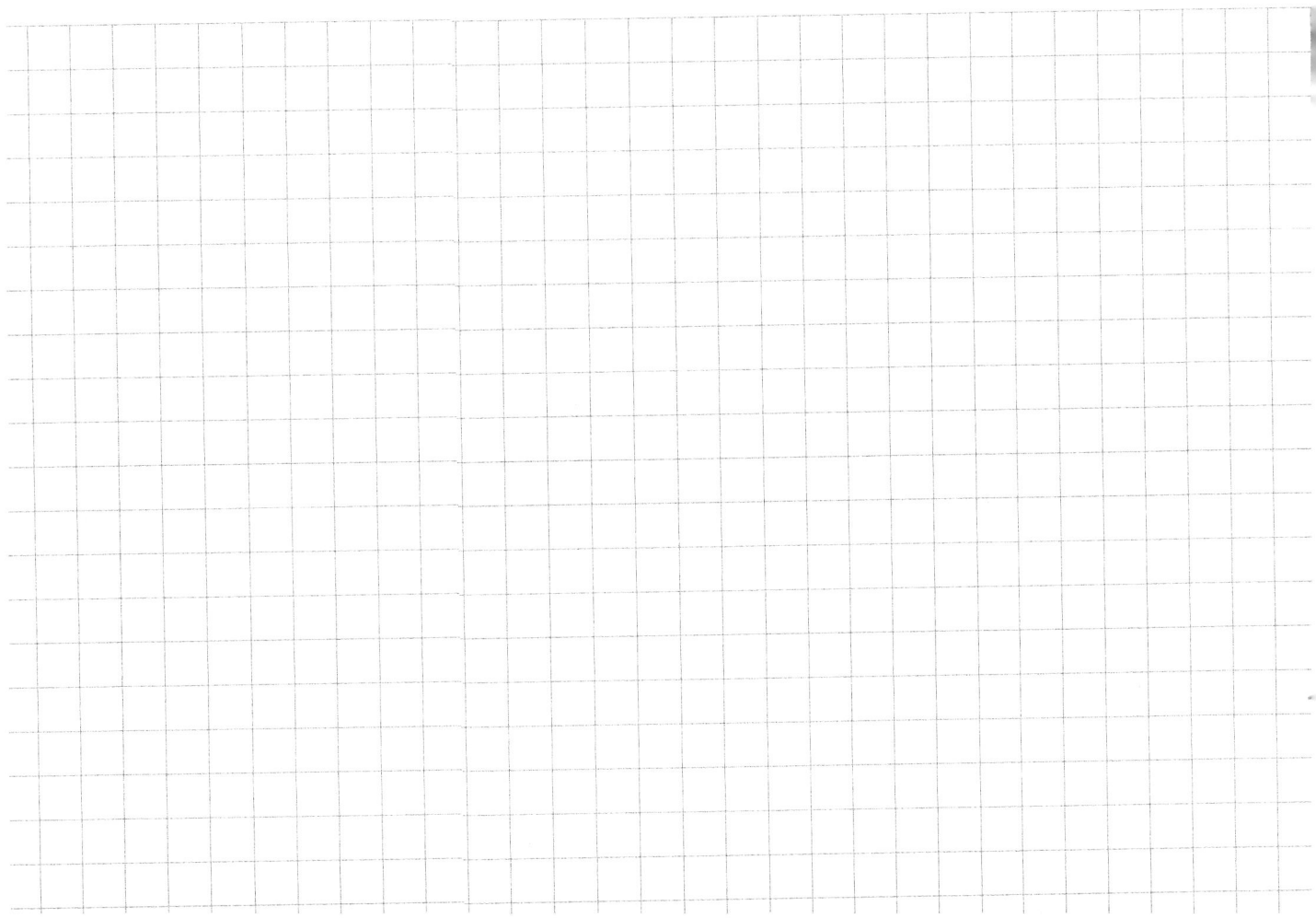

FINDER

Date		Day	
Start Time		End Time	
Location			
Temperature		Weather	

Sketch	Directions (N S *p f*)	Intensity Estimates	Key
			0 = extremely bright 1 = bright areas 2 = general hue of disc 3 = shading near limit of visibility 4 = shading well seen 5 = unusually dark shading

Instrument	Seeing (Antoniadi Scale) I II III IV V
Magnification	Filters: W#
Sky very bright bright fair twilight dark	Transparency very good good fair poor
Phase Estimate: % filter W#	Disc Diameter
Illuminated Disc	Unilluminated Disc

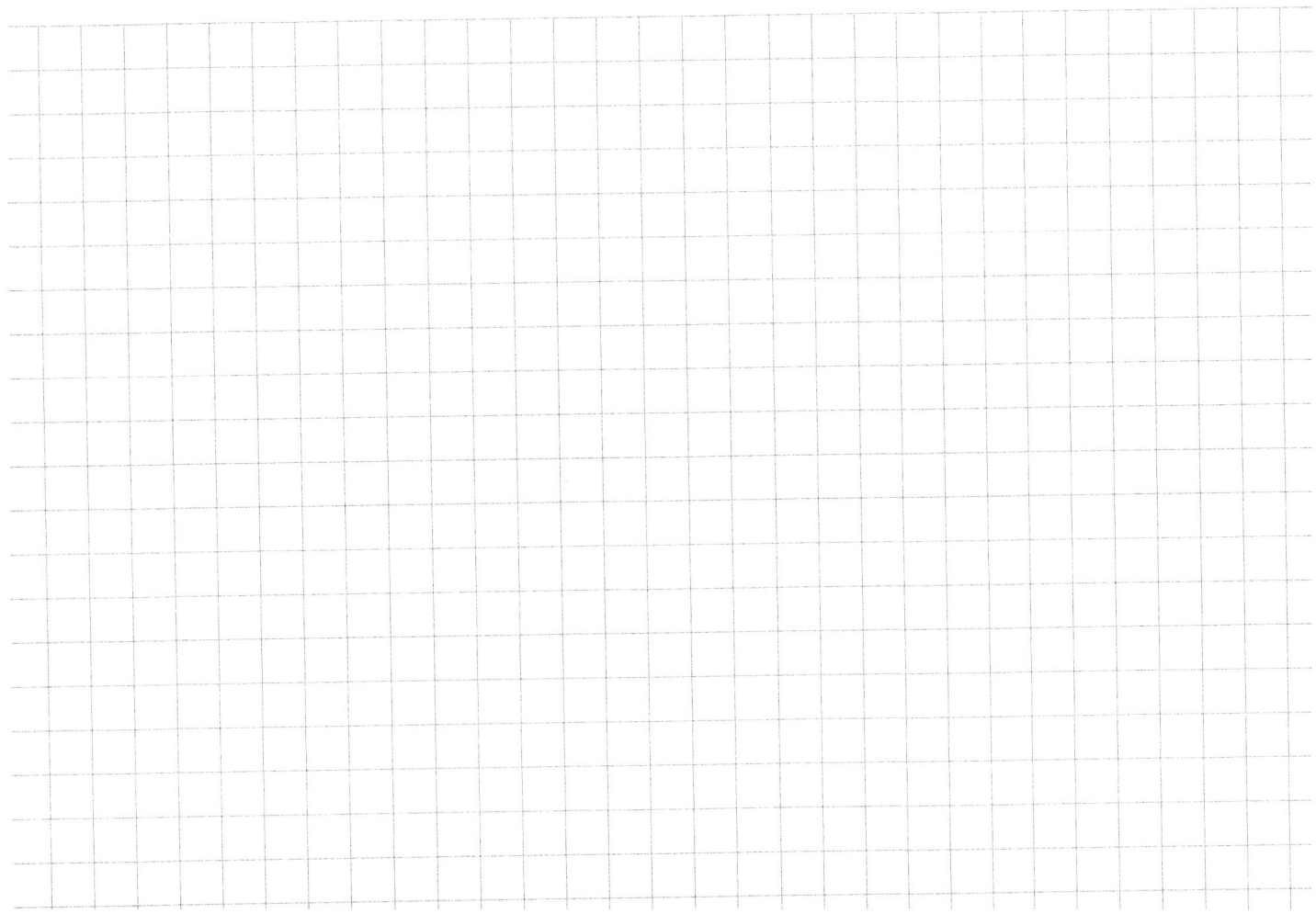

FINDER

Date	Day
Start Time	End Time
Location	
Temperature	Weather

Sketch	Directions (N S *p f*)	Intensity Estimates	Key
○	↕ ↔	○	0 = extremely bright 1 = bright areas 2 = general hue of disc 3 = shading near limit of visibility 4 = shading well seen 5 = unusually dark shading

Instrument	Seeing (Antoniadi Scale)
	I II III IV V
Magnification	Filters: W#
Sky very bright bright fair twilight dark	Transparency very good good fair poor
Phase Estimate: % filter W#	Disc Diameter
Illuminated Disc	Unilluminated Disc

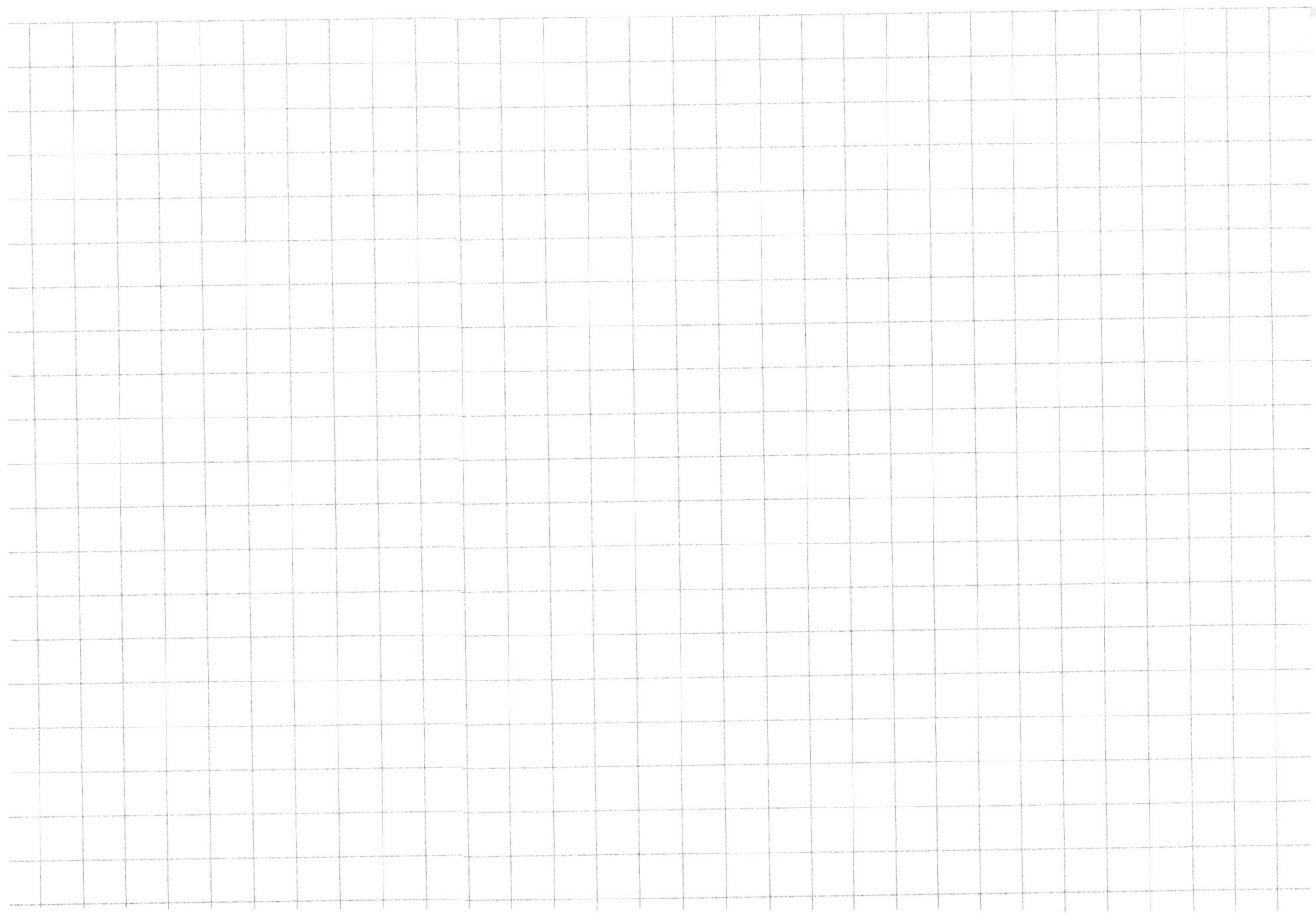

FINDER

Date		Day
Start Time		End Time
Location		
Temperature		Weather

Sketch	Directions (N S *p f*)	Intensity Estimates	Key
	↕ ↔		0 = extremely bright 1 = bright areas 2 = general hue of disc 3 = shading near limit of visibility 4 = shading well seen 5 = unusually dark shading

Instrument	Seeing (Antoniadi Scale) I II III IV V
Magnification	Filters: W#
Sky very bright bright fair twilight dark	Transparency very good good fair poor
Phase Estimate: % filter W#	Disc Diameter
Illuminated Disc	Unilluminated Disc

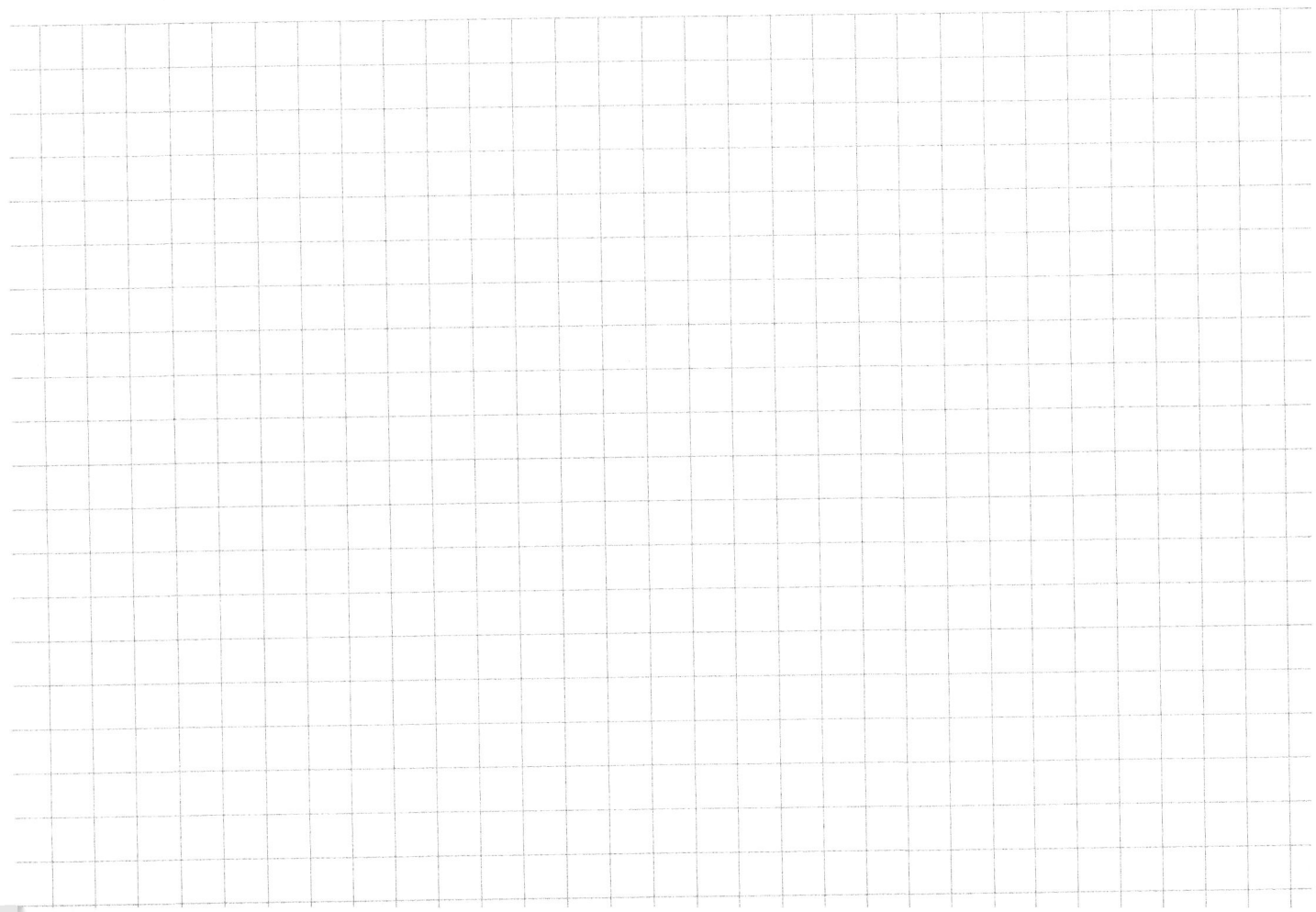

FINDER

Date	Day
Start Time	End Time
Location	
Temperature	Weather

Sketch	Directions (N S *p f*)	Intensity Estimates	Key
	↕ ↔		0 = extremely bright 1 = bright areas 2 = general hue of disc 3 = shading near limit of visibility 4 = shading well seen 5 = unusually dark shading

Instrument	Seeing (Antoniadi Scale) I II III IV V
Magnification	Filters: W#
Sky very bright bright fair twilight dark	Transparency very good good fair poor
Phase Estimate: % filter W#	Disc Diameter
Illuminated Disc	Unilluminated Disc

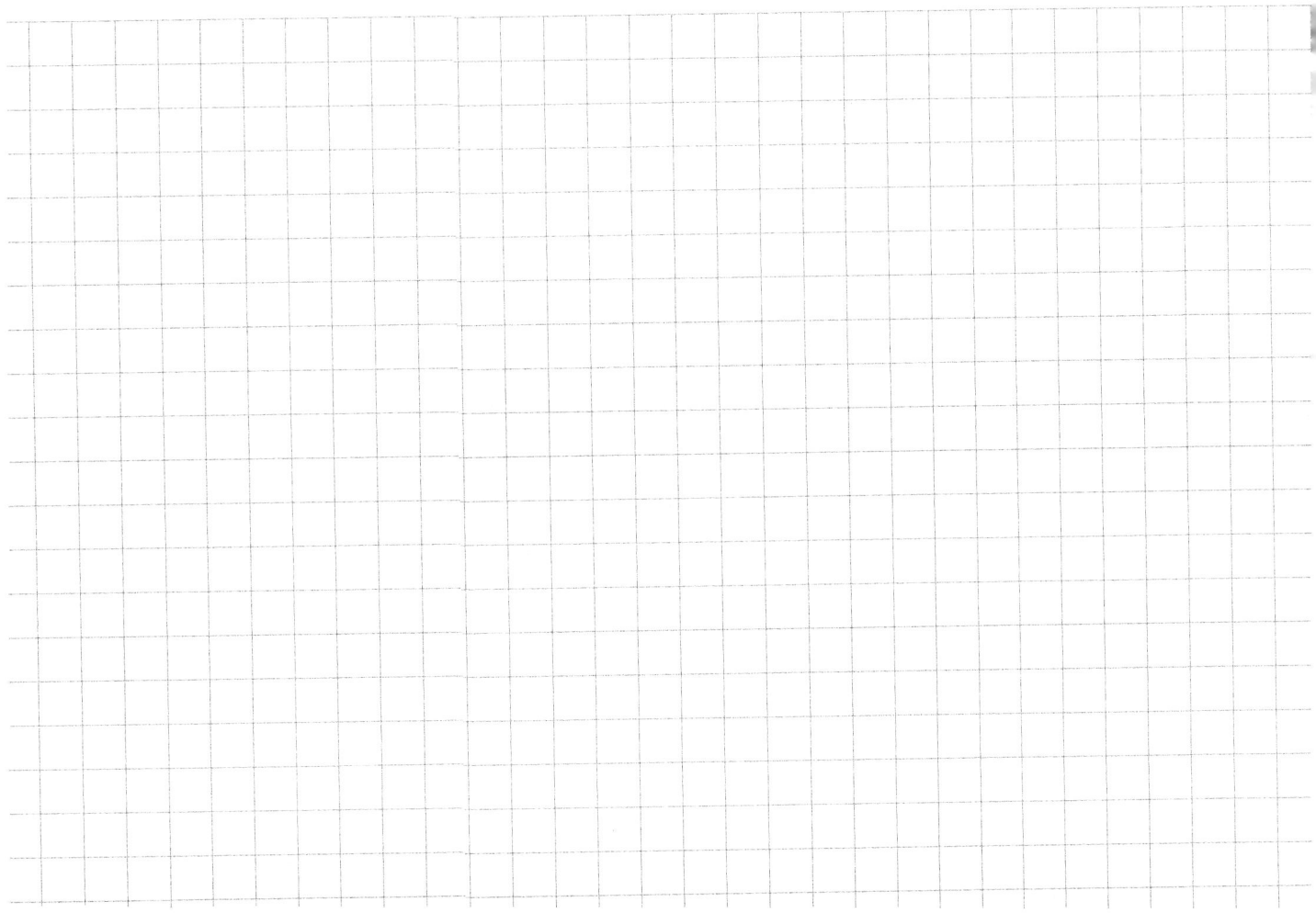

FINDER

Date	Day
Start Time	End Time
Location	
Temperature	Weather

Sketch	Directions (N S *p f*)	Intensity Estimates	Key
○	↕ ↔	○	0 = extremely bright 1 = bright areas 2 = general hue of disc 3 = shading near limit of visibility 4 = shading well seen 5 = unusually dark shading

Instrument	Seeing (Antoniadi Scale) I II III IV V
Magnification	Filters: W#
Sky very bright bright fair twilight dark	Transparency very good good fair poor
Phase Estimate: % filter W#	Disc Diameter
Illuminated Disc	Unilluminated Disc

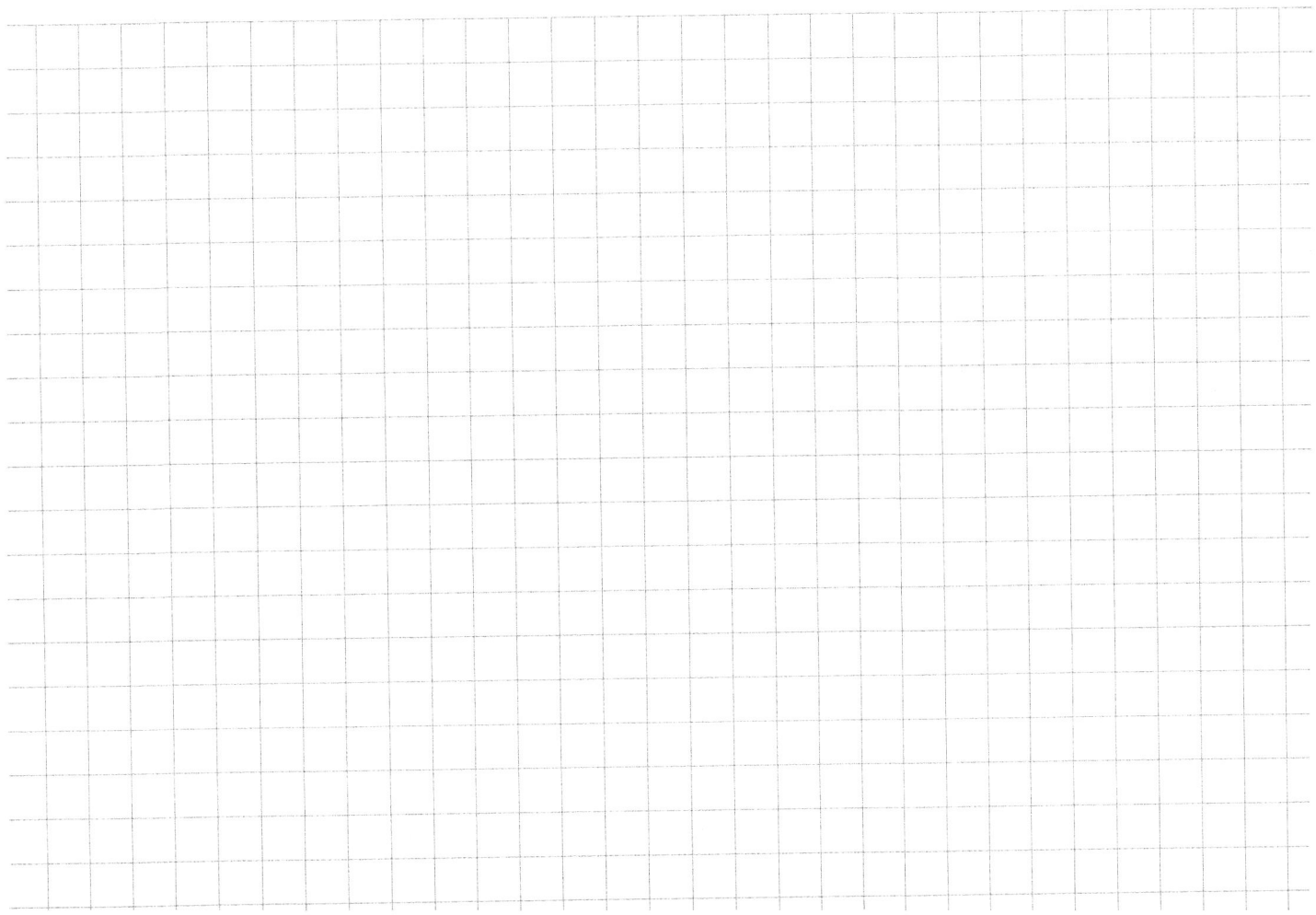

FINDER

Date		Day	
Start Time		End Time	
Location			
Temperature		Weather	

Sketch	Directions (N S *p f*)	Intensity Estimates	Key
	↕ ↔		0 = extremely bright 1 = bright areas 2 = general hue of disc 3 = shading near limit of visibility 4 = shading well seen 5 = unusually dark shading

Instrument	Seeing (Antoniadi Scale)
	I II III IV V
Magnification	Filters: W#
Sky very bright bright fair twilight dark	Transparency very good good fair poor
Phase Estimate: % filter W#	Disc Diameter
Illuminated Disc	Unilluminated Disc

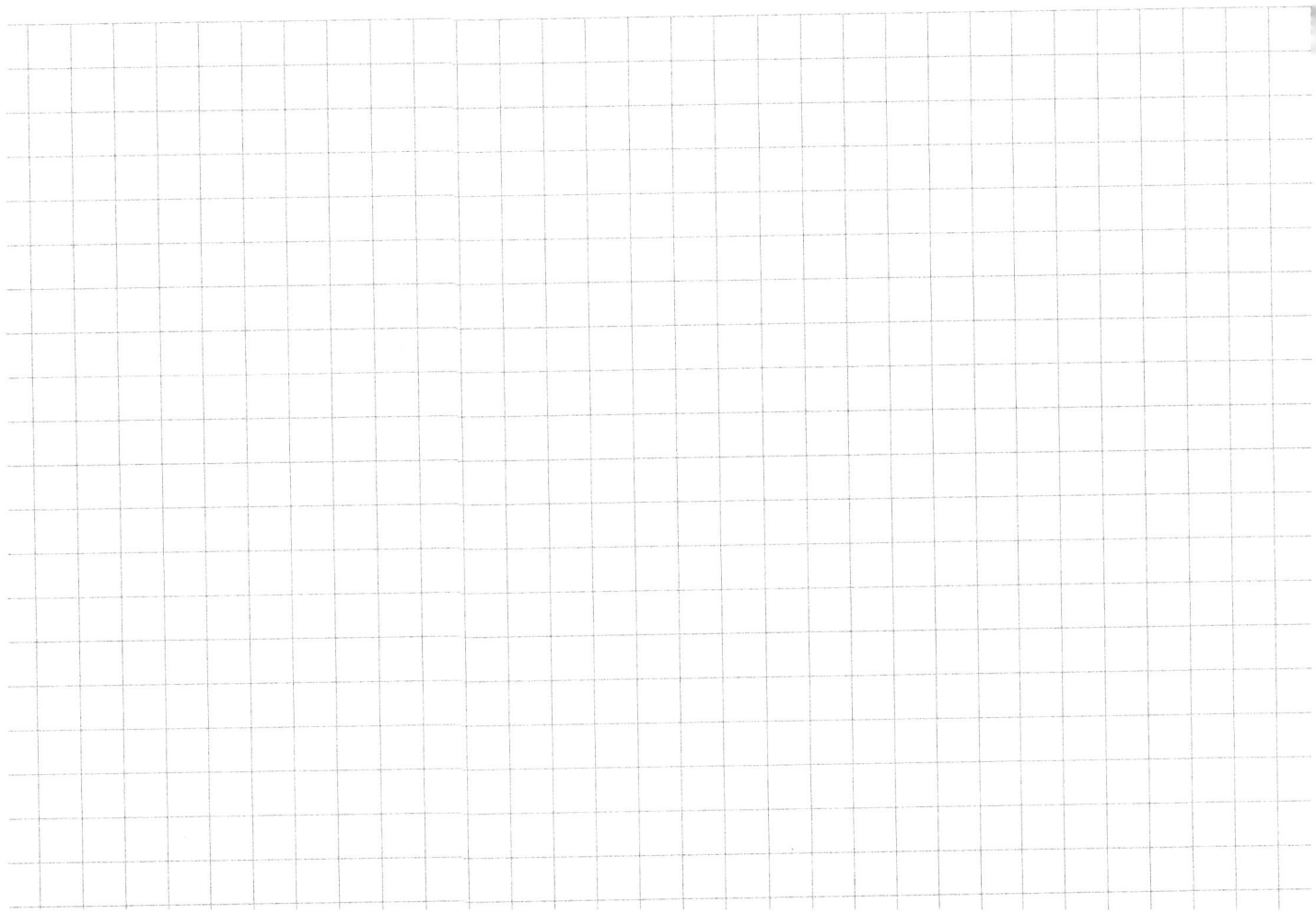

FINDER

Date		Day	
Start Time		End Time	
Location			
Temperature		Weather	

Sketch	Directions (N S *p f*)	Intensity Estimates	Key
			0 = extremely bright 1 = bright areas 2 = general hue of disc 3 = shading near limit of visibility 4 = shading well seen 5 = unusually dark shading

Instrument	Seeing (Antoniadi Scale)
	I II III IV V
Magnification	Filters: W#
Sky very bright bright fair twilight dark	Transparency very good good fair poor
Phase Estimate: % filter W#	Disc Diameter
Illuminated Disc	Unilluminated Disc

FINDER

Date		Day	
Start Time		**End Time**	
Location			
Temperature		**Weather**	

Sketch	Directions (N S *p f*)	Intensity Estimates	Key
			0 = extremely bright 1 = bright areas 2 = general hue of disc 3 = shading near limit of visibility 4 = shading well seen 5 = unusually dark shading

Instrument	Seeing (Antoniadi Scale)
	I II III IV V
Magnification	Filters: W#
Sky very bright bright fair twilight dark	Transparency very good good fair poor
Phase Estimate: % filter W#	Disc Diameter
Illuminated Disc	Unilluminated Disc

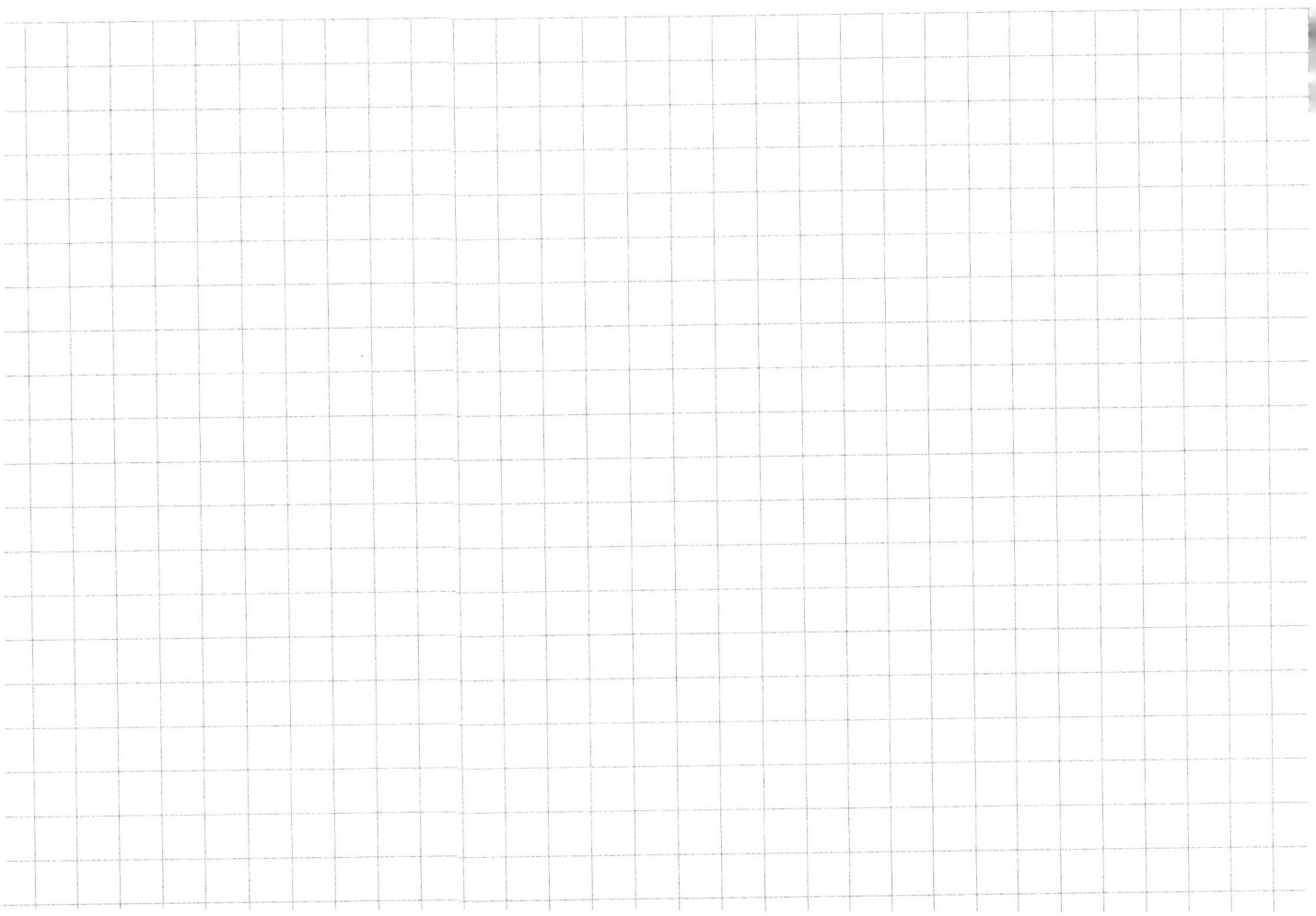

FINDER

Date		Day	
Start Time		End Time	
Location			
Temperature		Weather	

Sketch	Directions (N S *p f*)	Intensity Estimates	Key
	↕ ↔		0 = extremely bright 1 = bright areas 2 = general hue of disc 3 = shading near limit of visibility 4 = shading well seen 5 = unusually dark shading

Instrument	Seeing (Antoniadi Scale) I II III IV V
Magnification	Filters: W#
Sky very bright bright fair twilight dark	Transparency very good good fair poor
Phase Estimate: % filter W#	Disc Diameter
Illuminated Disc	Unilluminated Disc

FINDER

Date		Day	
Start Time		End Time	
Location			
Temperature		Weather	

Sketch	Directions (N S *p f*)	Intensity Estimates	Key
	↕ ↔		0 = extremely bright 1 = bright areas 2 = general hue of disc 3 = shading near limit of visibility 4 = shading well seen 5 = unusually dark shading

Instrument	Seeing (Antoniadi Scale) **I II III IV V**
Magnification	Filters: W#
Sky very bright bright fair twilight dark	Transparency very good good fair poor
Phase Estimate: % filter W#	Disc Diameter
Illuminated Disc	Unilluminated Disc

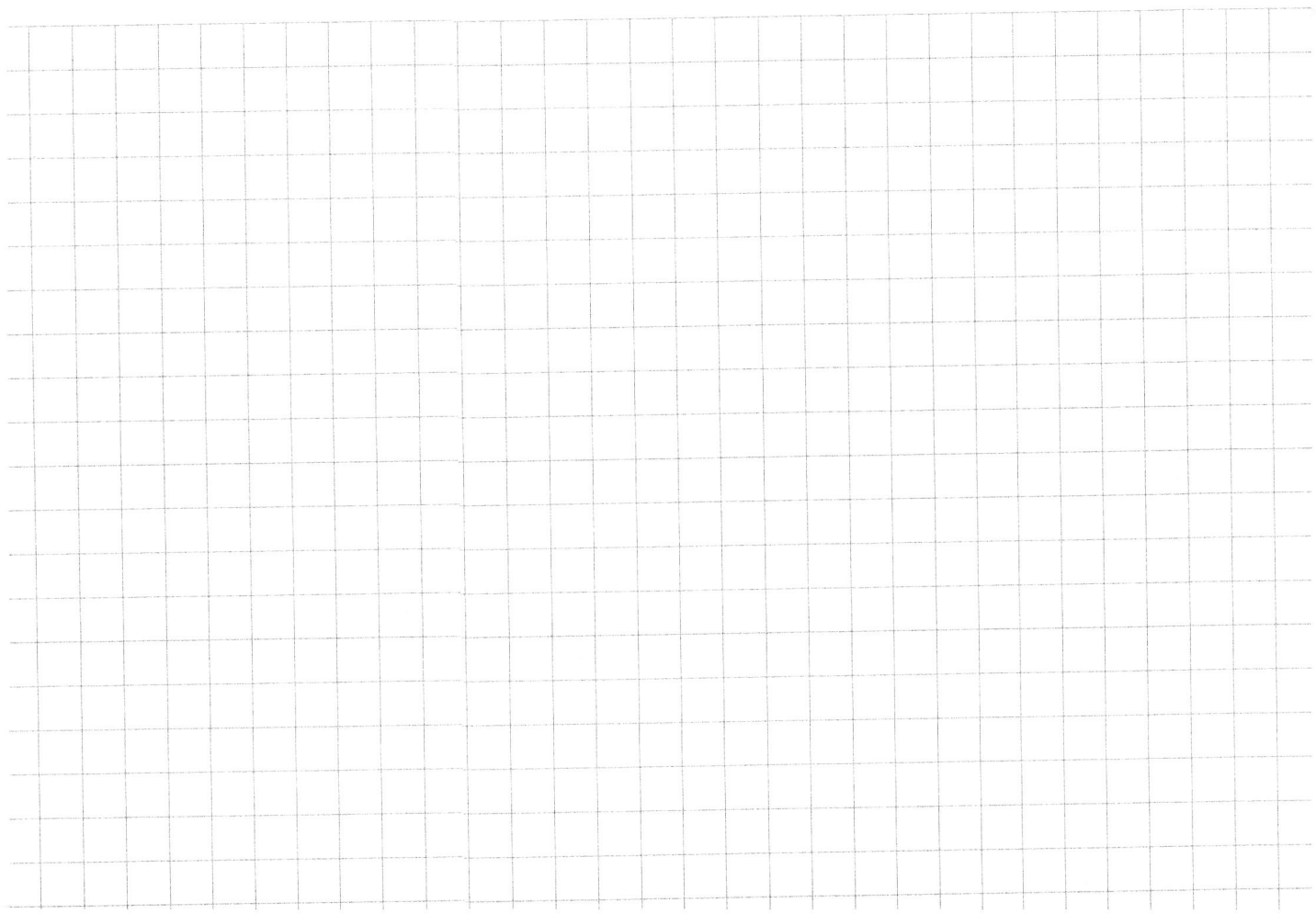

FINDER

Date		Day	
Start Time		End Time	
Location			
Temperature		Weather	

Sketch	Directions (N S *p f*)	Intensity Estimates	Key
	↕ ↔		0 = extremely bright 1 = bright areas 2 = general hue of disc 3 = shading near limit of visibility 4 = shading well seen 5 = unusually dark shading

Instrument	Seeing (Antoniadi Scale)
	I II III IV V
Magnification	Filters: W#
Sky very bright bright fair twilight dark	Transparency very good good fair poor
Phase Estimate: % filter W#	Disc Diameter
Illuminated Disc	Unilluminated Disc

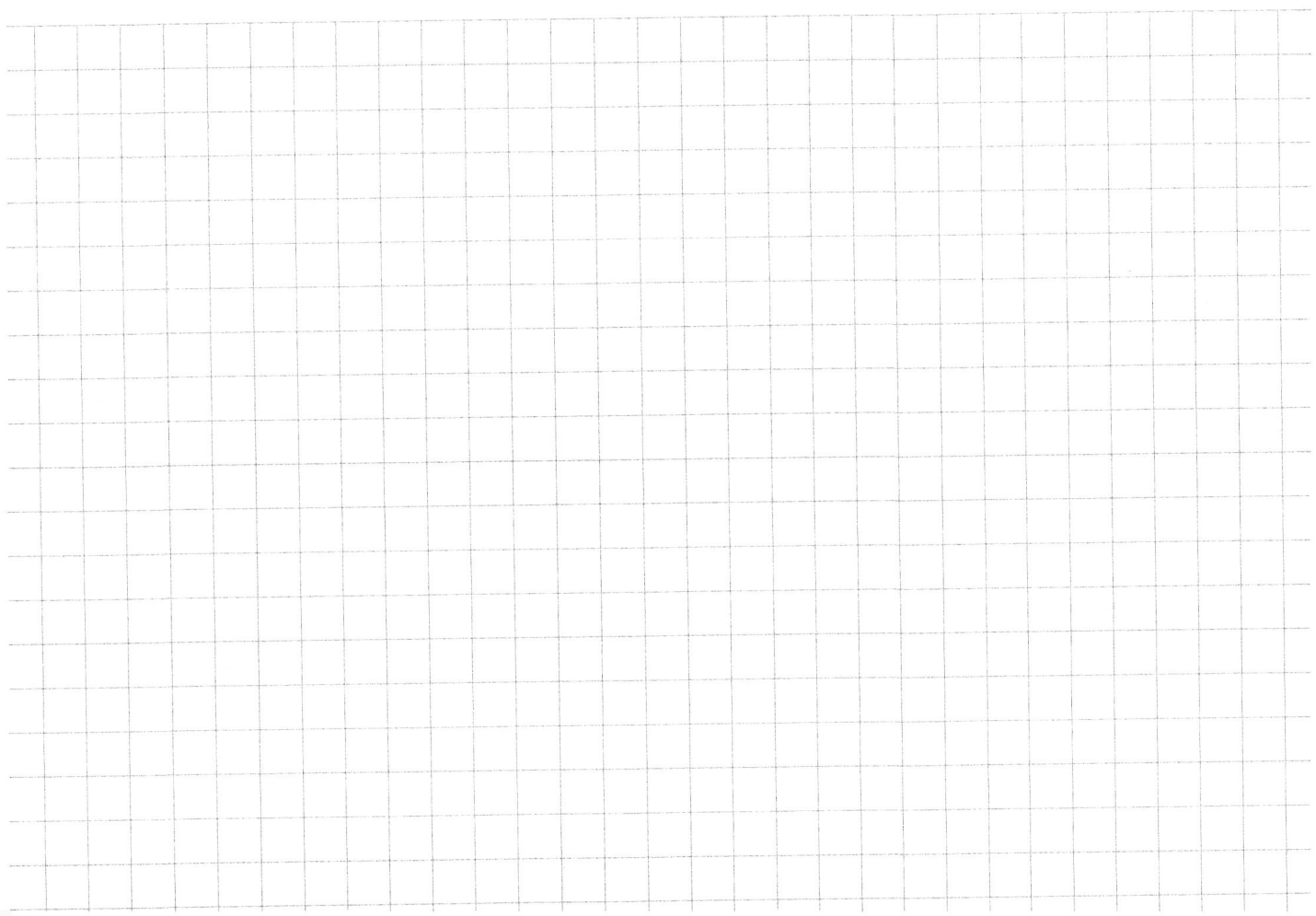

FINDER

Date	Day
Start Time	End Time
Location	
Temperature	Weather

Sketch	Directions (N S *p f*)	Intensity Estimates	Key
○	↕ ↔	○	0 = extremely bright 1 = bright areas 2 = general hue of disc 3 = shading near limit of visibility 4 = shading well seen 5 = unusually dark shading

Instrument	Seeing (Antoniadi Scale) I II III IV V
Magnification	Filters: W#
Sky very bright bright fair twilight dark	Transparency very good good fair poor
Phase Estimate: % filter W#	Disc Diameter
Illuminated Disc	Unilluminated Disc

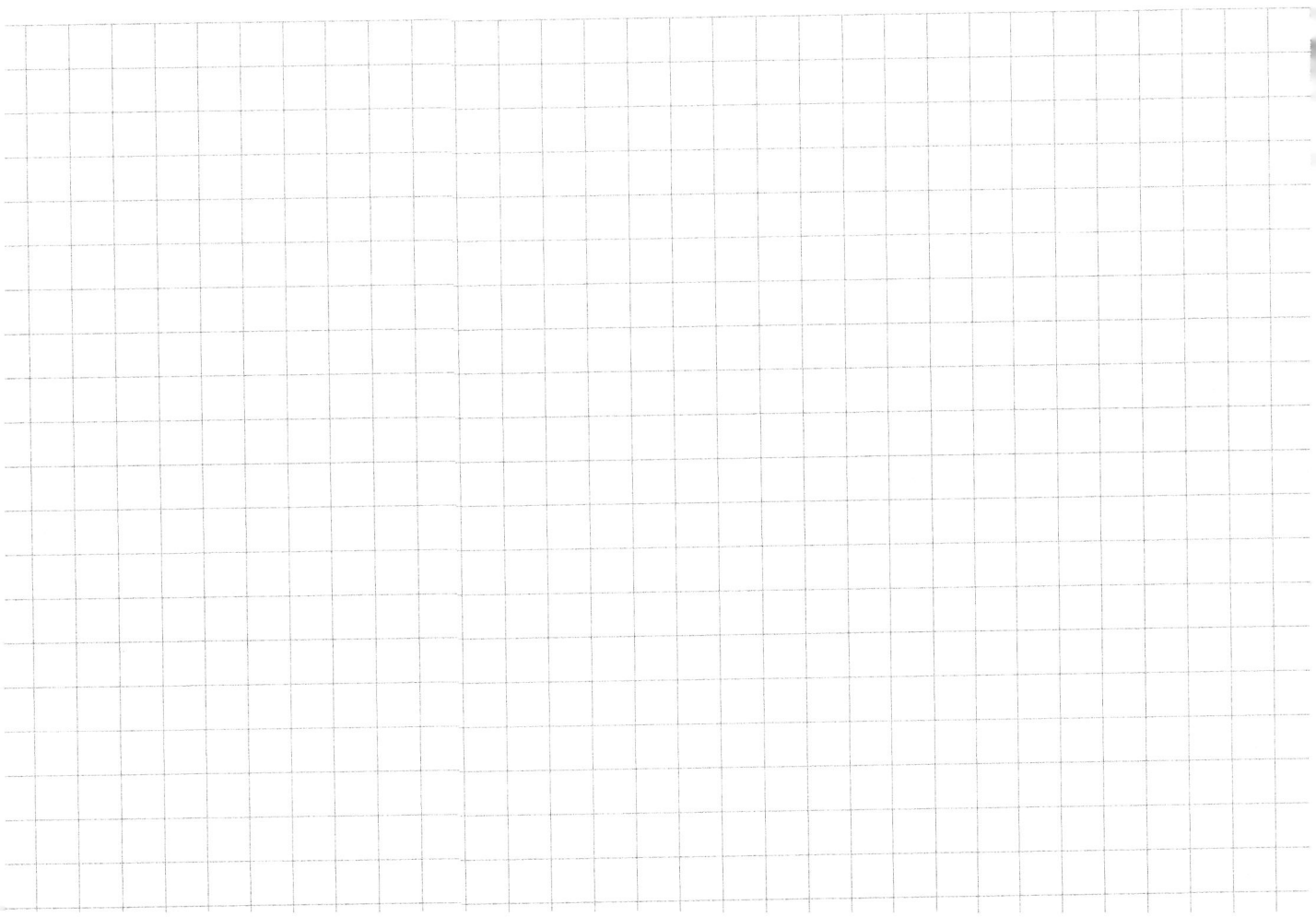

FINDER

Date	Day
Start Time	End Time
Location	
Temperature	Weather

Sketch	Directions (N S *p f*)	Intensity Estimates	Key
	↕ ↔		0 = extremely bright 1 = bright areas 2 = general hue of disc 3 = shading near limit of visibility 4 = shading well seen 5 = unusually dark shading

Instrument	Seeing (Antoniadi Scale) I II III IV V
Magnification	Filters: W#
Sky very bright bright fair twilight dark	Transparency very good good fair poor
Phase Estimate: % filter W#	Disc Diameter
Illuminated Disc	Unilluminated Disc

FINDER

Date	Day
Start Time	End Time
Location	
Temperature	Weather

Sketch	Directions (N S p f)	Intensity Estimates	Key
	↕ ↔		0 = extremely bright 1 = bright areas 2 = general hue of disc 3 = shading near limit of visibility 4 = shading well seen 5 = unusually dark shading

Instrument	Seeing (Antoniadi Scale) I II III IV V
Magnification	Filters: W#
Sky very bright bright fair twilight dark	Transparency very good good fair poor
Phase Estimate: % filter W#	Disc Diameter
Illuminated Disc	Unilluminated Disc

FINDER

Date	Day
Start Time	**End Time**
Location	
Temperature	Weather

Sketch	Directions (N S *p f*)	Intensity Estimates	Key
	↕ ↔		0 = extremely bright 1 = bright areas 2 = general hue of disc 3 = shading near limit of visibility 4 = shading well seen 5 = unusually dark shading

Instrument	Seeing (Antoniadi Scale) I II III IV V
Magnification	Filters: W#
Sky very bright bright fair twilight dark	Transparency very good good fair poor
Phase Estimate: % filter W#	Disc Diameter
Illuminated Disc	Unilluminated Disc

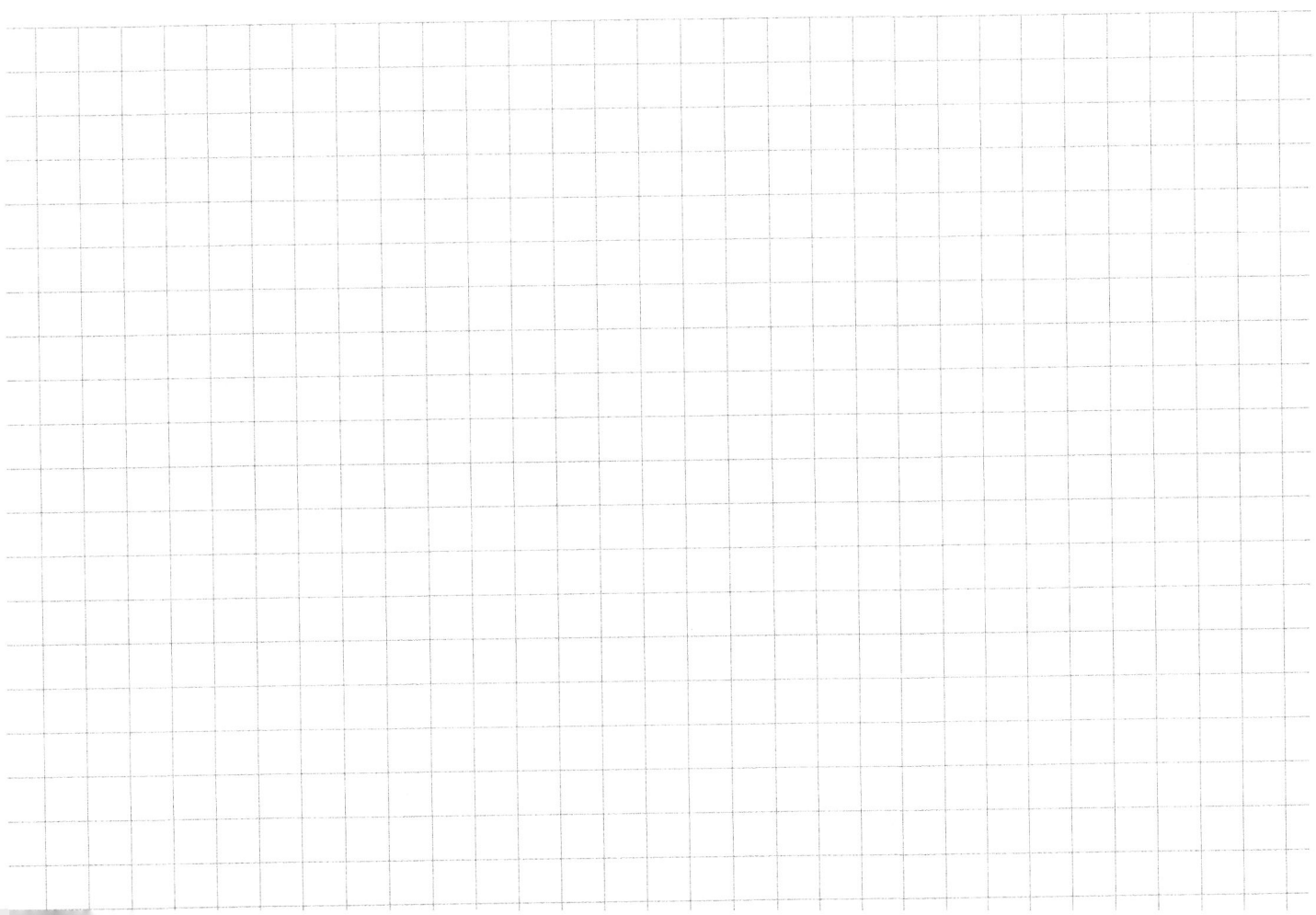

FINDER

Date		Day	
Start Time		End Time	
Location			
Temperature		Weather	

Sketch	Directions (N S *p f*)	Intensity Estimates	Key
	↕ ↔		0 = extremely bright 1 = bright areas 2 = general hue of disc 3 = shading near limit of visibility 4 = shading well seen 5 = unusually dark shading

Instrument	Seeing (Antoniadi Scale)
	I II III IV V
Magnification	Filters: W#
Sky very bright bright fair twilight dark	Transparency very good good fair poor
Phase Estimate: % filter W#	Disc Diameter
Illuminated Disc	Unilluminated Disc

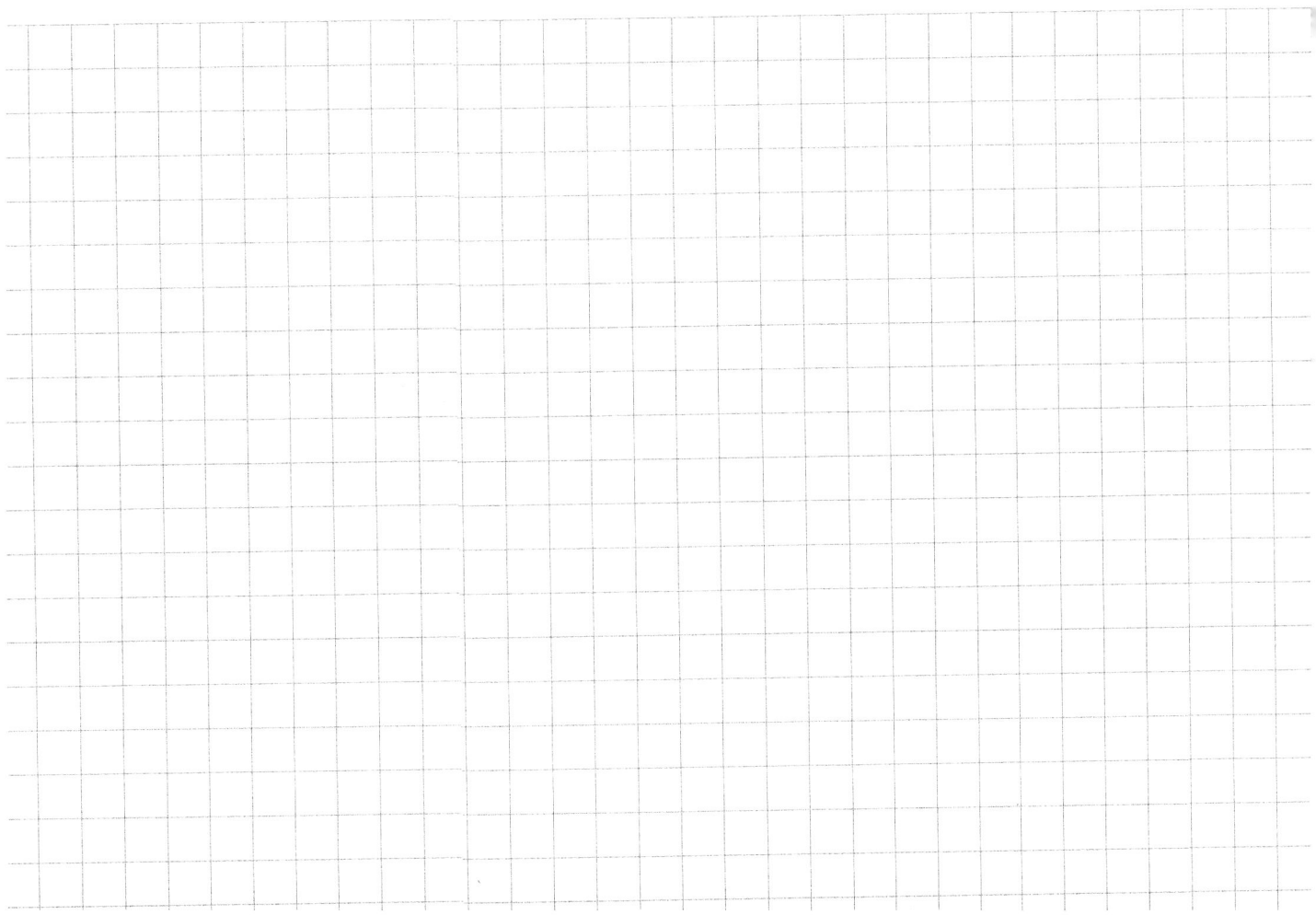

FINDER

Date	Day
Start Time	End Time
Location	
Temperature	Weather

Sketch	Directions (N S *p f*)	Intensity Estimates	Key
			0 = extremely bright 1 = bright areas 2 = general hue of disc 3 = shading near limit of visibility 4 = shading well seen 5 = unusually dark shading

Instrument	Seeing (Antoniadi Scale)
	I II III IV V
Magnification	Filters: W#
Sky very bright bright fair twilight dark	Transparency very good good fair poor
Phase Estimate: % filter W#	Disc Diameter
Illuminated Disc	Unilluminated Disc

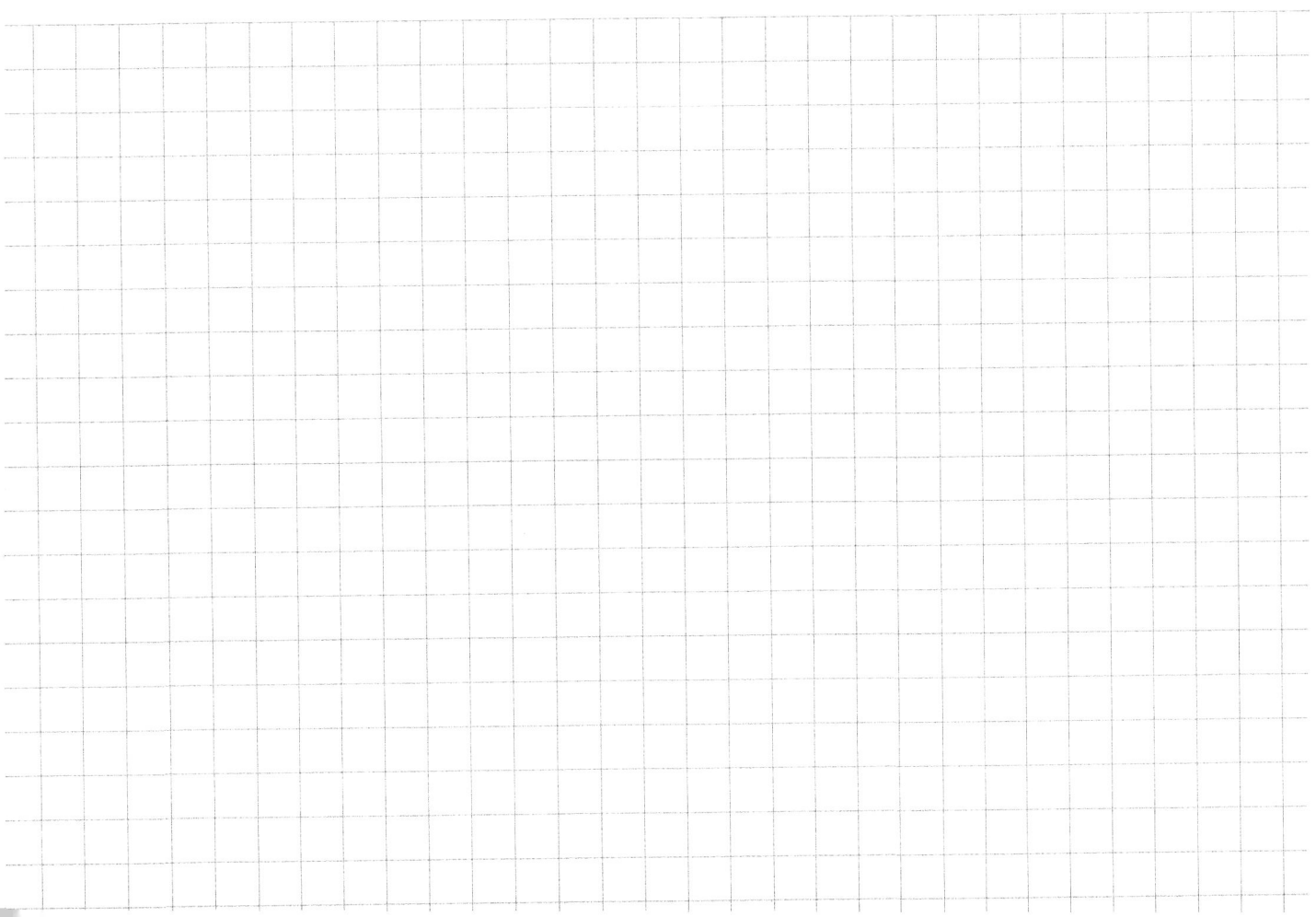

FINDER

Date		Day	
Start Time		End Time	
Location			
Temperature		Weather	

Sketch	Directions (N S *p f*)	Intensity Estimates	Key
	↕ ↔		0 = extremely bright 1 = bright areas 2 = general hue of disc 3 = shading near limit of visibility 4 = shading well seen 5 = unusually dark shading

Instrument	Seeing (Antoniadi Scale) I II III IV V
Magnification	Filters: W#
Sky very bright bright fair twilight dark	Transparency very good good fair poor
Phase Estimate: % filter W#	Disc Diameter
Illuminated Disc	Unilluminated Disc

FINDER

Date	Day
Start Time	End Time
Location	
Temperature	Weather

Sketch	Directions (N S *p f*)	Intensity Estimates	Key
			0 = extremely bright 1 = bright areas 2 = general hue of disc 3 = shading near limit of visibility 4 = shading well seen 5 = unusually dark shading

Instrument	Seeing (Antoniadi Scale)
	I II III IV V
Magnification	Filters: W#
Sky very bright bright fair twilight dark	Transparency very good good fair poor
Phase Estimate: % filter W#	Disc Diameter
Illuminated Disc	Unilluminated Disc

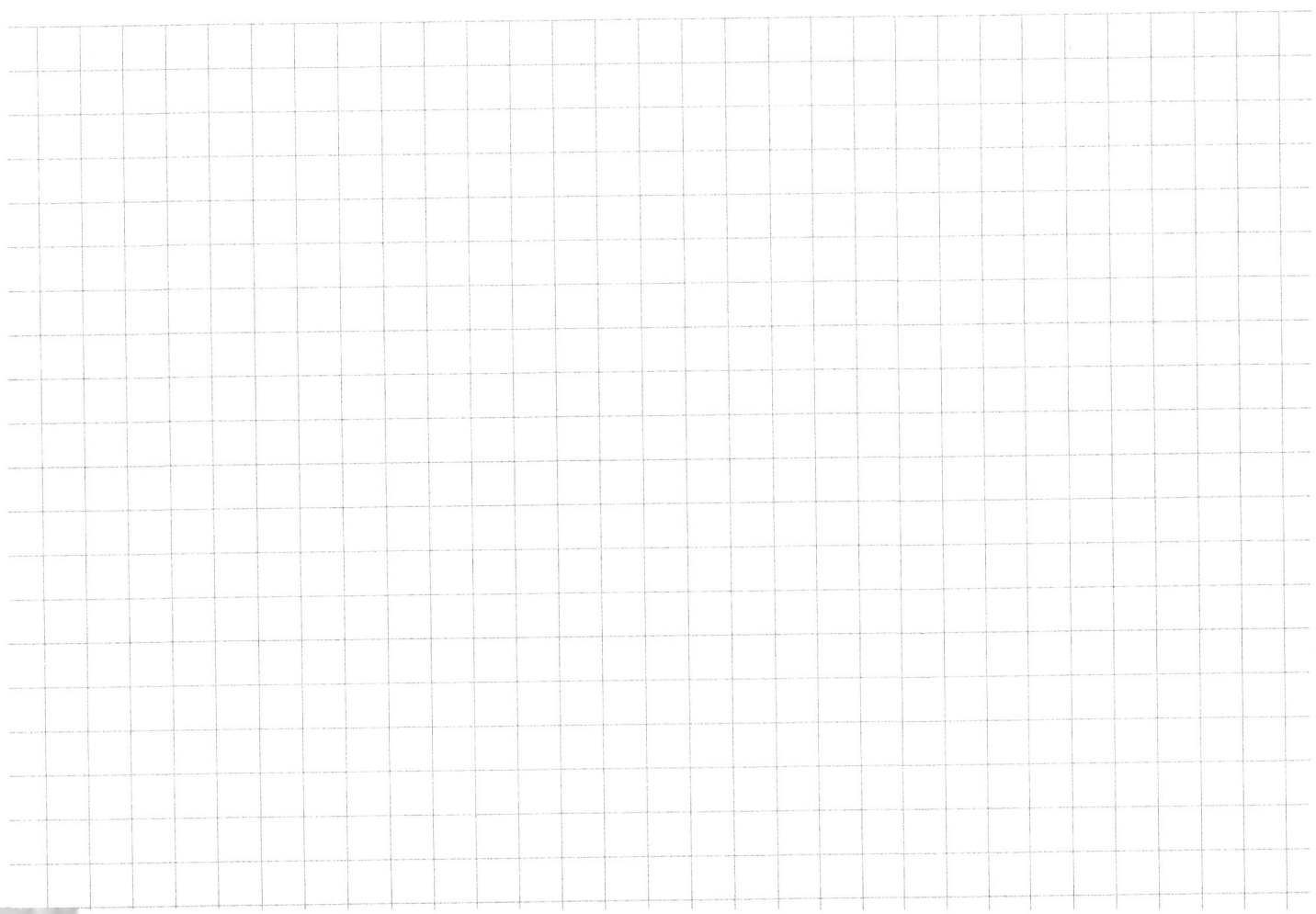

FINDER

Date	Day
Start Time	End Time
Location	
Temperature	Weather

Sketch	Directions (N S *p f*)	Intensity Estimates	Key
	↕ ↔		0 = extremely bright 1 = bright areas 2 = general hue of disc 3 = shading near limit of visibility 4 = shading well seen 5 = unusually dark shading

Instrument	Seeing (Antoniadi Scale)
	I II III IV V
Magnification	Filters: W#
Sky very bright bright fair twilight dark	Transparency very good good fair poor
Phase Estimate: % filter W#	Disc Diameter
Illuminated Disc	Unilluminated Disc

FINDER

Date		Day	
Start Time		End Time	
Location			
Temperature		Weather	

Sketch	Directions (N S *p f*)	Intensity Estimates	Key
	↕ ↔		0 = extremely bright 1 = bright areas 2 = general hue of disc 3 = shading near limit of visibility 4 = shading well seen 5 = unusually dark shading

Instrument	Seeing (Antoniadi Scale)
	I II III IV V
Magnification	Filters: W#
Sky very bright bright fair twilight dark	Transparency very good good fair poor
Phase Estimate: % filter W#	Disc Diameter
Illuminated Disc	Unilluminated Disc

FINDER

Date		Day	
Start Time		End Time	
Location			
Temperature		Weather	

Sketch	Directions (N S *p f*)	Intensity Estimates	Key
	↕ ↔		0 = extremely bright 1 = bright areas 2 = general hue of disc 3 = shading near limit of visibility 4 = shading well seen 5 = unusually dark shading

Instrument	Seeing (Antoniadi Scale)
	I II III IV V
Magnification	Filters: W#
Sky very bright bright fair twilight dark	Transparency very good good fair poor
Phase Estimate: % filter W#	Disc Diameter
Illuminated Disc	Unilluminated Disc

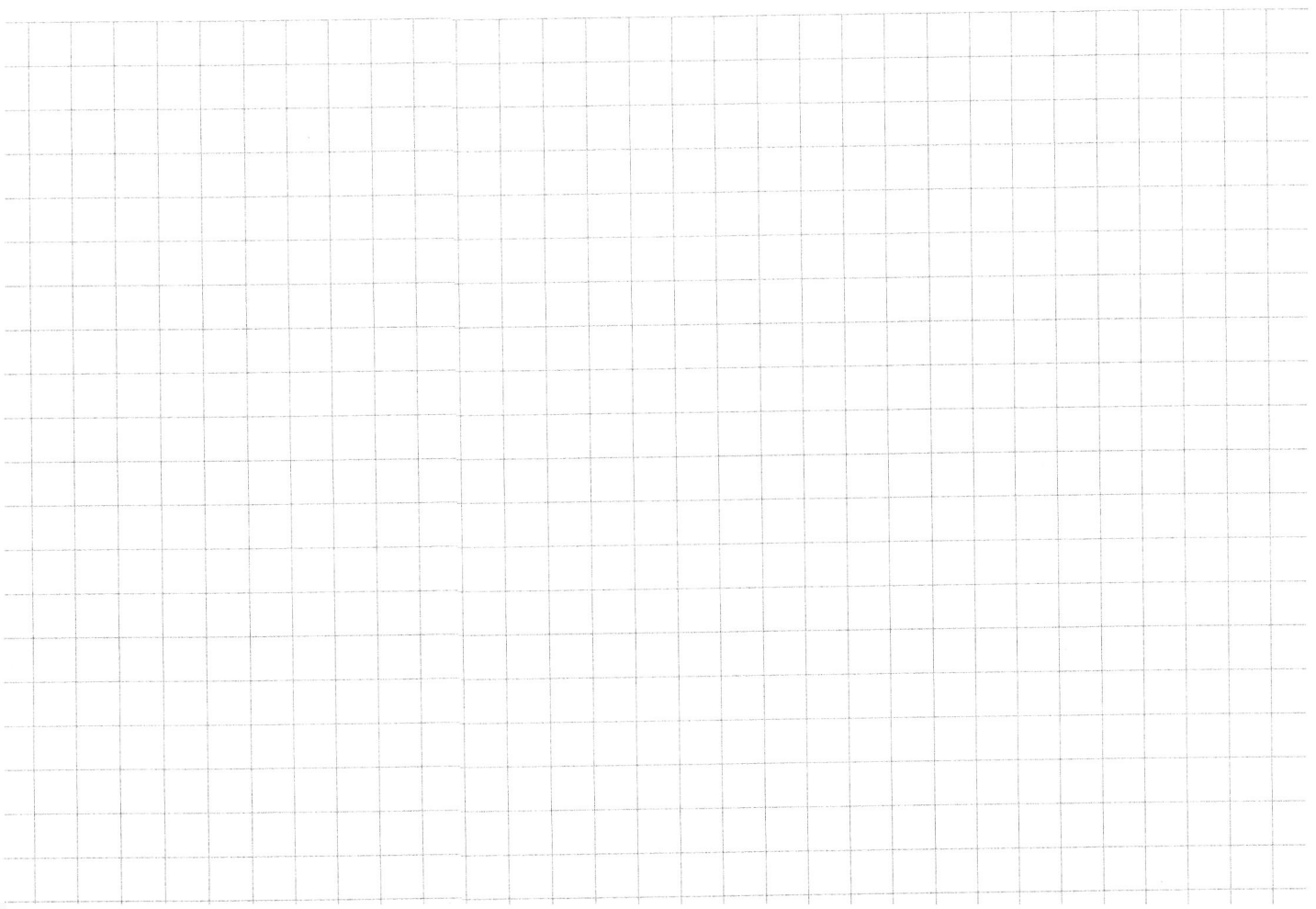